C. L. EASTON
STRANGERS OF THE NIGHT

Cover Design: Black Pirate Book Covers

Editing: J Shaw

Publisher: Black Rose Publishing

Ebook ISBN: 978-1-778782-8-6

Paperback ISBN: 978-1-7782968-6-4

NOTE FROM THE AUTHOR

This book ends on a cliffhanger...

Take warning this is a dark romance. Our leading lady doesn't choose between her lovers (lucky bitch)

It includes:
Graphic sexual explicit scenes, physical assault, bullying, raw sex/sex without a condom, bondage, temperature play/ice play, public sex.
Everyone is over the age of eighteen, none of the characters are blood related.

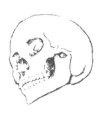

When you love Halloween so much you needed to write a book, then you stumble upon a porn scene that needed to be included in said book.
Happy reading.

PLAYLIST

Another Life- Motionless in White
Bury a Friend- Billie Eilish
Monsters- All Time Low, blackbear
The American Nightmare- Ice Nine Kills
Hells Bells- AC/DC
Am I Evil?- Metallica
Voices- Motion in White
Already Dead- Hollywood Undead
This Means War- Avenged Sevenfold
Courtesy Call- Thousand Foot Krutch
My Name is Mud- Primus

Find more on Spotify- Strangers of the Night cleaston

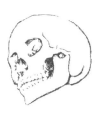

I

CATALINA

Halloween night.

The one time of the year where the residents of Eastwood let loose.

No questions asked. The only night that I can do what I do without having to look over my shoulder. See this town is known for two things. It's university and the other I don't think it's well known, but they have a Halloween purge night. I'll tell you about that later. I thought when I enrolled in Eastwood University that I would be financially stable, turns out that's a bunch of bullshit. I had to find work, your scholarship only covers the bare minimum. I struggled for the first couple of months before my professor noticed. He told me about an opportunity that I would enjoy.

Now at first, I didn't think I would enjoy it so much, but being a loner at this school I didn't have a problem. I really don't have many friends. Okay, I don't have any, so my evenings are always available. After showing me the first time, I was hooked. I started digging graves and making a profit from my professor. Cadavers are a much-needed thing in the medical training.

Not the most glamorous job, but when you are working on a low income in an expensive town, you need to supplement everything. I'm gathering up my gear to head out for the night. I'm told there are three bodies that need to be brought into the school. It'll be an all-night job. *Thank God.* I don't think I can handle all the drunk shenanigans, or any of the shenanigans going on tonight.

I change into my uniform, which consists of leggings, my black t-shirt with my skull lovers on it. I'm classy. Grabbing my combat boots, I set them by my front door. Before I remember.

"Ah, shit."

I dart back into the kitchen to find my satchel can't forget about this. I have all my important things in there, like snacks. After strapping on my boots, I head out to my 1976 Volkswagen Beetle, my baby. I call her Johnny. Don't worry, no dead bodies will ever go in her. Can you imagine trying to get that smell out of the upholstery? No thanks. Luckily, I have a van parked at the campus for everything else.

Evening is upon us, the streets are lined with jack o lanterns, every yard decorated to the max with decorations. I pity those that aren't it'll be a free for all having your house destroyed. That's why I'm glad I live in my shitty ass apartment building. Plus, when I'm finished for the night, I can lock myself away from all this bullshit that's beginning to fill the streets with teens and adults, dressed up in costumes chasing each other, drinking and having fun.

This town is by far the *weirdest*. "I'll never understand this town," I whisper out loud.

As I near the campus, I pull in the parking lot. I park behind the shed by the east side of the medical department. The last thing I need is someone figuring out what I've been doing this past year. I race across the parking lot without getting caught by any frat boy. That's the last thing I need tonight is getting caught in one of their sick orgy games. That's the thing about this night. The mayor has sick fantasies, and this is a way of saying it's not cheating. Once inside, I pull my phone out, checking which cemetery I need to hit up first. Eaglewood it is. It's the furthest one out. It's only one body. The other two are in Eastwood Cemetery which is in the middle of town.

I feel relieved to be leaving town even if it's only for a short while. I know it won't last long. Digging up one body won't be long enough for the silence. It gives me time to think, like how a group of guys that go here are not the friendliest. Three of them to be exact. Dorian, Nyx, and Cole. They get pissed off every time I pass them in the halls. I can't figure out what I did for them all to hate me so much. I only share one class and it's with Nyx. I pray to God I don't run into either of them tonight.

Eaglewood Cemetery gives me the creeps, and that's saying a lot considering I live for this sort of thing.

Huge iron gates welcome you as you drive down the road. Oak trees guard the property everywhere you look. Guarantee they are over a hundred years old. Both sides of the road are lined with tombstones and mausoleums. Leaves that have fallen are now gathered against each tombstone. Fall is such a beautiful season, except for this night. Like I said Eastwood is fucking weird. I never understood why they went all *purge* like on this night. Well, in a way I do, but to involve the whole town.

Following the directions to the new grave I find it over a hill towards the back, I'll have to walk to get to it, grabbing my bag off the front seat I jump out of the van, heading to the back I swing open the doors. I'm greeted with a beautiful sight. All my things are neatly placed in Rubbermaid containers on the left side. I take my shovel to begin with. I'll come back for everything else later.

Do I feel guilty for digging bodies up? No. I probably should, but it's not like I'm doing anything horrible to them. Their bodies are technically being used for good, even if they never wanted it to. We all make sacrifices, even when we are dead.

The nice thing about fresh graves, the soil hasn't had time to be compacted. It only takes me a couple of hours to dig. The best thing about this school, the gym. Can you imagine me doing this with noodle arms? I grab a baby wipe from my bag so I can wipe some dirt off my hands. I can't stand dirty hands. I also can't stand wearing gloves. It's a vicious cycle. I take a body bag, my hooks and a crowbar from the van. This is the part that gets tricky, and where I sometimes wish I had an extra person. Before I do anything further, I make sure no one is around. I don't trust this night no more than any other night. When I'm only greeted with silence, I continue. Wrapping a bandana around my face, I grip my crowbar as I stare down into the hole that's housing a dirty coffin. With a deep breath, I jump back down.

I'll save you the nitty gritty. After opening the casket, I prep the body for hauling it upwards. I know this is a lot for a five-foot-two little old me. Remember, I've been doing this for a year now, so it's all repetitive motion, plus my professor only gives me certain bodies that he thinks I can handle. Climbing out of the hole, I lay out the body bag getting ready for the hardest part. Now I'm no physics major, but with no leverage this is taking the longest.

"Fuck me, Joe, why are you so heavy? How much shit did they stuff you with?"

Sweat pours down my back, my biceps are ready to give out, and I'm panting like a bitch in heat. This body is heavier than I expected. With a few more tugs, their feet are finally above ground. I plant my hands on my knees to try to regain my breath. No need for cardio, I get plenty of it. After what feels like a lifetime, I zip up the bag. It's time to drag Joe all the way back to the van. My favourite gigs are when I can park closer. But that's also me being extremely lazy. Opening the doors, I step inside to drag the body bag inside, with one final pull, I get it into the van. I slam the door shut, resting my back against them, I wipe the sweat off my forehead letting out a deep sigh. I take a deep inhale of the night's crisp air. Closing my eyes, I take a few minutes to enjoy the silence because we're headed back to crazy town. I wish every night was like tonight, there's just something about Halloween that makes my soul happy. It's too bad it doesn't last longer than one night, I wished I lived somewhere different from this place. I open my eyes glancing at Eastwood in the distance, guess I better get this done with.

I'm barely in town, when the streets are littered with more people running in every direction. It's the most I've seen by far. Said jack-o-lanterns are now smashed everywhere. Soon crime will be ridden come midnight, that's when the gangs fall amongst the town. The time that I need to be somewhere other than outside. Those three that I spoke of earlier, they belong to the gang The Soul Stealers. How you might ask that I know this. It's rather fucking easy. They make it well known around campus.

I've kept my bandana on with my dark hair in a messy bun. My disguise working for now, making my way back to the school, I need to unload before heading to the other cemetery. The east side of the school is still vacant. Guess no one wants to hang around here tonight. Backing up to the loading dock I get out and unlock the doors. I find a gurney in one of the anatomy labs. I wish I had more room in the van for one of these. Once the body is loaded, I wheel it back to the lab, placing it in the cooler. With a heavy breath, I begin the toughest job of the night.

Travelling down main street, it's eerie. A couple trash cans are set on fire letting me know the gangs are coming out, everyone is running around yelling and chasing each other. I see a small crowd gathering around the alley entry and chances are it's a small orgy going on. Shop owners take precautions of their businesses and board everything up, but that won't stop most people. I hit the brakes as a group of clowns dash out in front of me. One hits the hood of the van and waves his bat at me. My heart jumps in my throat, but luckily they run off towards the park. Once I'm inside the cemetery, I'll be safe. I repeat this until I believe it. I hear motorcycles in the distance growing louder. I hit the accelerator, like hell I'm getting caught in that shit. I make one last turn and I'm here. Dark stone pillars with wrought-iron fence the entire perimeter, large gargoyles loom overhead guarding all that live here now.

Too bad two of their residents will be leaving. I know what you're thinking. *Jesus Cat, don't you have a fucking heart.* I do. But she's black as the darkest of night. I wasn't always the normal kid growing up, so I was built to be tougher, guess I was a little too tough because I don't care what happens anymore. I prefer the dead over the living, they at least can keep all my secrets to themselves. Never spilling anything while I bitch to them about this miserable life I'm living.

I park next to a mausoleum, so I can read over my text. I need to make sure I'm in the right area.

Sometimes everything looks all same especially at night. Third on the left, but it's the fourth down. That doesn't make any fucking sense to me. Looks like I'm not driving any further after all. There are rows and rows of mausoleums down here. I just wanted a quick night. *Fuck.* It's getting late, I knew I should've waited for these two until tomorrow. Digging took a little longer than I expected tonight.

The motorcycles revving is a steady sound in the distant, I don't think they would come here because why would they. I'm the only one here. No one ever hides out with dead things. They are all out looking for someone to shack up with or causing small riots on main street with the gangs. Giving my head a shake, I get back to work. I don't have time to worry about everybody else's business. I have other pressing matters to worry about. Like finding this stupid grave. I'll have to come back for the last one. Making the last turn I finally see the fresh grave.

As I'm digging, I feel like I have eyes on me, but that's insane. I've checked this area over occasionally, to make sure I'm alone. I haven't seen or heard a peep out of anything. Even the animals don't want to be out. I can't shake the feeling though, and my skin is crawling by the time the hole is finished. Once the body bag is laid out, I can't take it anymore. I crouch low and take in the cemetery. It's a cloudy night, thankfully the moon is hidden letting me become invisible as well. I scan what I can take in the mausoleums, not seeing anyone or thing. Squinting in case I missed any reflection, nothing. My mind must be finally catching up with me. I jump back into the hole, attaching the hooks around the body's armpits.

"I'm sorry for what I'm about to do," I mumble. Then I climb out of the hole.

As I have the body halfway out, crunching of leaves have me halting my movements.

"Fuck," I whispered.

I slowly turn my head to see what is coming up behind me, my heart is jumping in my chest when more leaves crunch. My biceps twitch from holding a body for longer than I've ever have before. If gotta do this for longer, I'm going to drop this poor thing. Would they notice if I lower it back down? I'll take my fucking chances. Inch by painful inch, I lower it back down. Every time I do I pause, I can hear male voices to the left of me in the distance. I won't have time to clean and run. My best bet will be to dump and run and pray. It'll be a huge loss, but once someone knows I've been here, I can't come back. I'm done for. I calculate the risk and say fuck it.

I take off like a bat out of hell. I make it halfway to the van when I hear them yell at me.

"Hey, where the fuck did you come from?"

"Get her!"

"I'll cut her off."

Oh, I don't think so. Digging into my pocket I find my keys. I know how this works; I'm not getting caught without being prepared. I can see my van in the distance. So, fucking close, I can hear the pounding of their boots quickly gaining on me. Guess I need that cardio after all.

"I'll, call the cops on you fuckers," I yell over my shoulder.

The sad thing is the cops won't do anything tonight and we all know it. I'm just wasting my breath. Once I'm caught, I'm caught. I stumble over a rock and tumble to the ground. I wince in pain when I smack my head on a tombstone. That's going to cost me time. I scramble to my feet taking off again.

I didn't stand a chance. As a body slams into me from out of nowhere. His arms wrap around me, a scream leaves me as we fly. We tumble on the ground with me landing on the bottom. All the air in my lungs evaporating leaving me gasping. Whoever landed on top of me wasn't getting off anytime. As I try to suck air into my lungs, I got a look at the prick who landed on me.

What my eyes land on isn't what I was expecting. He's wearing a black hoodie with the hood up with a LED mask covering his face, in lime green. When I look around, two more bodies come into view dressed the same way, the only difference are their masks. One is red, the other is blue.

That's how I know I'm in deep fucking trouble.

2

CATALINA

The moment I laid my eyes on all three of them, I could feel the energy radiating off them. I knew I was in trouble. I'm thankful to be still wearing my bandana, my identity still hidden from whoever these three are.

The one wearing the red mask started laughing suddenly.

"Well, look what we caught for the night boys. Fresh meat and no one around to save her." His voice is muffled from behind his mask, so I couldn't even figure out who he is if I wanted too.

The one on top of me shifts slightly, letting me get a deep intake of air into my lungs finally. He looks down at me, if only I could see his facial expression. His head tilts to the side, when his hand move to my forehead a spike of pain shoots before fading to an dull ache.

"You're bleeding, don't move."

Why he would care is beyond me. He reaches for his back pocket of his jeans, he pulls out a white paisley printed bandana. That's kinda gross if you ask me. I try to move my head away from him, but he holds my head still. Going about cleaning my cut.

"Seriously dude, who gives a fuck if she's bleeding or not." The one in Red says. He's been a real dick this whole time. "She's only here for one reason tonight."

"I know it's a hard concept, but head wounds bleed a shit ton, and I don't need blood everywhere. So, if you don't mind, I'm going to get it to stop before we do anything further."

Well, so much for being a gentleman. The Blue masked one hasn't said a single word. He's stands taking the entire scene in. I can only imagine the questions he has formed and I ain't telling him shit. It's Halloween, so figure it out.

"Get her up, we only have a couple of hours left and I'm not wasting anymore time."

"Yeah, whatever. Don't worry I didn't forget that you're in charge."

After the Green mask hauls himself up, his hand clamps around my upper arm, hauling me upwards. The world spins for a second before my body can catch up. My eyes ping between all three of them. Red stands the tallest, he's also the hugest. His hoodie is pulled tight around his muscles. Green looks to be a few inches shorter, although muscular he doesn't compare. His body felt solid while on top of me, and I'll admit it felt wrong to be turned on when he shifted his growing bulge into my needy pussy. I know he felt something because when he reached for his bandana; he shifted forwards more than needed. I had to stifle a moan in. They don't need to know how turned on I am for them. That's the last thing I need for them to know. Especially on this night. We all have a secret fantasy. *Okay.*

Now Blue is a mystery. He hasn't come any closer to where he currently is, so I'm assuming he's around the same height as Green maybe taller. They are strangers of the night, after all. Do I really need to get to be besties with them? I need to get away from them and get the fuck home. I still have my keys in my hand, I need a better opening to run.

"What do you want from me? I don't want anything to do with this night." I try to plead with them, hoping it'll be enough for them.

They all laugh, including Blue. His deep voice sending tingles through my body.

"I think you can guess, and I think you know Catalina," Blue says, with venom in his voice.

My entire world shifts, how the fuck do they know me? I made sure to stay hidden tonight without running into anyone. This doesn't make sense. Green slowly lowers my bandana, giving away my facial expressions to them all.

"H-How do you know my name?"

Red only shrugs, not giving away anything. So does the other two. Wrenching my arm in Green's grip I try to get free, his hand only tightens. Causing a small whimper to slip past my lips.

"Don't worry, you know us. We aren't quite strangers." Red speaks. His words bringing some relief to my over racing brain.

"I don't understand any of this. How did you know where I was?"

"Let's just say, we've been watching you for a long time now. Tonight, made the perfect opportunity to make our move," Green speaks into my hair. Almost nuzzling close to me.

With a steady breath, I stomp as hard as I can on his foot. His hold on me breaks and I bolt. If they want me, they can work for it. I'm closer to the van than I thought. Their voices behind me yelling at me to stop. Like fuck, I'm listening to them. I've never been more nervous than I am right now with adrenaline coursing through your body. It makes it hard to unlock anything, especially this van that will help me get away. I wish this van was equipped with remote locks, but she's older than time. My hands shake as I struggle to get the key in the hole, I can't hear anything besides the pounding of my heart. My breathing is coming in pants. I finally get the key in only for another body to slam me into the van, pressing me flat up against the door panel.

"Didn't get very far did we half pint?" Red whispered in my ear.

"Don't fuckin' call me that, you cunt." I elbow him in his hard abdomen. A small grunt come out of him making me smile. "Serves you right, jackass."

He runs his finger along my neck, goosebumps ripple along my skin. The only reaction I have is wanting to curl my toes, and to see where else he'll touch me. I can't let them know the effect they have on me. My body on the other hand, is a traitor.

"What's wrong half pint, mad because you can't get away from us? Or mad because you like what we do to you?"

"I don't know what you're talking about," I hiss at him. "Don't fuckin' touch me again." I try jerking my head away from him, but it's hard when he has me pinned, pressing into me. His laugh vibrates against my back.

"Tell yourself what you need to, but you're not getting away from us. You'll be with us tonight. You can't outrun us. Your body wants us, no matter how much you lie to yourself."

That's when Blue comes close, taking the keys from my hand. His fingers gently caress over top of mine, giving me a calming effect. Red hauls me out of the way, while the doors get unlocked. Green rounds the back of the van producing a set of zip ties. My heart stills.

"You don't need those; I swear I'll behave." Swallowing the large lump that settled in my throat, they all stare at me. I can tell they don't want to take any chances, but neither do I. I don't want my hands restrained. Before I can argue anymore, Red tugs my arms behind my back. My breath hitches, the second the ties touch my skin. I try to suck as much air as I can, but it's not helping. My mouth fills with extra saliva as bile creeps up my throat, I try to swallow multiple times, so I don't throw up everywhere. I can't focus on anything other than trying to calm myself down. The last time I had a huge panic attack was when I left home, that was almost two years ago. I thought I had everything under control again. It isn't until my vision starts to fade, I know I was in trouble. The pounding in my ears only grow louder by the second. When my knees buckle, large hands grab me around my biceps.

"Shit, maybe this wasn't such a good idea, man."

"It's a little late for that don't ya think? Open the fuckin' door."

Their voices are muffled, and I couldn't tell who was talking. Strong arms lift me up carrying me bridal style. I'm pretty sure it's Red, I can't help but rest my head on his chest. My entire body is spent of energy, and I lost my fight. My chest is still tight when I try to suck deep breaths in. It isn't until he places me inside of my van that the tears start. My night is sealed.

"Don't worry half pint. You're safer with us, if you believe it or not."

I find that hard to believe considering I have no idea who the fuck they are. They could be my worst nightmares and I'm walking to death's door right now. Yet I feel safe, and I can't explain it. How fucked up is that? It's not until he closes the door, that the other door closes too and I'm alone with Blue.

"You'll have fun with us tonight."

I don't say anything. I close my eyes and pray that this night goes by fast. It's only for the night, I can do this. I've lasted the other Halloweens yet this one is turning into a nightmare, how fair is that.

Turns out home, isn't my home. That would've been a dream. The house that stands in front of me is a black three-story Victorian that screams to my soul. How is it they live where I'm meant to be? This place is calling to me.

"Wow."

"Amazing right? Come on Wednesday, I think you'll enjoy what we have in store for you."

I highly doubt that, especially the way I'm feeling now. He helps me out of the van, that's when I hear the bikes nearing the house. I haven't looked around; my eyes are still fixed on this gorgeous house. Hands land on mine giving me a tug backwards. My back collides with a solid chest. Their hand runs up my ribs brushing alongside my breasts, causing a moan to fall from my lips.

"You like that, don't you, half pint?"

At the sound of his voice, I pull away. "Untie my hands, maybe I will."

"That's okay, I rather like restrained. Gives me more control of your body." He tugs the zip ties again, causing my heart to skip a beat.

"Please, untie me," I whispered.

"One way to get over a fear, is to face it," he whispers in my ear. He guides me towards the house, when we reach the porch, I halt my moves. "Don't be scared, we'll take care of you."

I see Blue and Green enter the house, leaving the door open for us. Red's hands wrap around my waist making me move into the house of horrors.

When I step inside, it nearly blows me away. The interior is dark like the outside, to the left of the front door stands a set of stairs leading to the second floor. To the right of me is the living room furnished with leather couches. Everything is so organized and kept clean. For a house filled with guys, I'm shocked. I'm led to another room further into the house, my body is buzzing with anticipation yet I'm nervous at the same time.

"All the way, stand in the middle," Red told me.

When I turn around, I'm greeted with such temptation. All three stand there, each dressed in jeans, black hoodie and a mask. I still don't know who they are.

"She listens well, I'm impressed. Kneel." Green's voice comes out husky.

His voice makes my pussy throb the most, it's already wet. I'm certain my panties are ruined. Kneeling the best, I can. I look up at them.

"Good girl," Blue said. Walking towards me, palming his growing bulge.

Sweet Jesus, that's turning me on even more.

"Tell me, have you ever done anything adventurous in bed before?"

I dip my head; he cups my chin lifting my head. My eyes stare into the blue cross stitches over his eyes on his mask.

"No need to be ashamed. We're not here to judge you."

With a deep breath. "I've only done the usual stuff I guess."

The other two-step forward creating a circle around me. "We'll take things slow then, guide you into it."

"Into what?"

"This, you do want this don't you? I can read your body like it's an open book, Catalina. Don't lie. How bad do you want to taste us?" Who knew the quiet one, is always the freakiest one? Blue runs his thumb over my bottom lip, my eyes close loving the way my skin tingles at his touch. He pushes his thumb, past my lips, into my mouth.

"Suck," he demands.

I hollow my cheeks sucking, then stroking him with my tongue. He pulls out giving me a groan.

"Please say you want this, Wednesday. I'm desperate to have you."

"Only for the night, right?" I look at all of them, they eventually nod. I swallow the lump I have stuck in my throat. "Yes, I need you all. Please."

3

CATALINA

All three of them undo their zippers. I grow wetter with each passing second waiting for what's in store. I've never done anything this crazy before and I can't believe I'm doing this. When I look over at Green, he's gripping his cock. Red's cock is hanging out, already half hard. Waiting for me, when I look back at Blue, his cock is beautiful. I've never seen one like his before, his cock has a Prince Albert plus a pubic piercing. My pussy tightens at the thought of what pleasures it'll bring.

Red threads his hand in my hair releasing it from the hair tie. Wrapping my hair around his hand, he tilts my head back.

"Open wide for him." Blue takes control of the group.

With no hesitation I open for him, he takes a hold of his large cock lining it up with my mouth. Holding my head still gives him all control. I'll be the first to admit, I'm not that experienced with giving head. He doesn't seem to care; he groans the deeper he goes. He's too large for me to fully take him, when he hit the back of my throat, I gag around him.

"Mmm, just like that baby. Take it all."

He continues to thrust his hips; my eyes water the harder he goes. I spread my knees apart for more balance or to take some relief off my sensitive clit. I need something, anything. He pulls out of my mouth, when Green steps up. He strokes himself letting out a frustrated groan.

"Stick your tongue out for me."

Opening wide, I stick my tongue out. He slaps my cheeks with his cock, whipping his pre-cum all over me.

"Such a dirty girl aren't you? How bad do you want his cock?" Blue asked, while walking behind me. "Tell me and I'll reward you."

"I want it so bad; I can taste it. Please."

"You heard her. Give her what she wants."

Blue wraps his hand in my hair, while Green slides his cock into my mouth. I wrap my lips around him. Blue's other hand runs down my body working towards my waistband of my leggings. I let out a moan when his thumb caresses my stomach going inside my thong. Green grunts when Blue moves my head forwards. I take over the movements. Moving until my nose touches his trimmed pubic hair. Pulling back on a gag, I take a deep inhale. As Blue's finger inches over my clit circling it. The sensation of both is overwhelming. His finger dips lower.

"So wet for us aren't you Wednesday. Enjoying yourself, are we?"

"Mmm hmm," I mumble around Green's cock. I continue bobbing as Blue's finger enters my slick core bringing me closer to my waiting orgasm. I clench my inner muscles around him. Closing my eyes as he strokes my g-spot. I can feel it nearing when he pulls his hand out of my pants. I whimper at the loss, I snap my eyes open. Green pulls out of my mouth, backing away.

"You've been a good girl, should we get you out of these clothes?" Blue grabs my wrists causing me to wince in pain. Coolness of a knife touches my wrist; with a flick, my hands are free.

I bring them forwards giving them a small rub. His hands run down my arm reaching for the hem of my shirt, he pulls it over my head. My nipples pebble under all their stares, even though I can't see them I know they're looking. I'm sitting in my black lace bra waiting. My entire body is on fire. Red extends his hand for me, placing my hand in his. I notice how his completely encloses around mine. You know what they say about large hands. Well, it's true ladies. Cause I still can't take my eyes off his girthy cock. Swallowing the excess saliva, he pulls me up. This is it. No turning back. I'm allowed one night of craziness, right? It's not like I'll ever see them again.

"Are we doing this in here? I'm about ready to blow," Red tells the other two.

"Might as well, she's ready." Green agrees, while pumping his cock.

I lick my lips while watching him. Why is that such a huge turn on. The sight alone makes my knees weak.

"Do you have any hard limits?" Blue asked.

I turn to face him, I bit my lip, while narrowing my brows. "Um. I don't know what you mean?"

"Okay, for example. Fisting, breath play, double vagina or double penetration, spanking." He finishes speaking and my jaw drops. What in the Satan have I gotten myself into. Fisting? That's a pass. I don't need them to explain it, I can take a wild guess. I'm also fond of breathing.

"The first two are a no." I try to say it with determination, but I'm sure my voice quivers at the end.

"That's okay. We have safe words in place, anytime you don't feel safe or need to stop. Use them. We'll stop immediately. Yellow means slow and red means stop. Understand?" Blue informs me of everything.

"Please don't tie my hands anymore, that's a huge red for me."

He nods, I look at the other two and they nod. I'll never tell them why, it's none of their business.

"Take your pants off. I want you in nothing but your underwear."

There is something about Blue that I want to figure out, if only I had time. Untying my boots, I kick them off. Dipping my thumbs into my waistband, I bend all the way down dragging them along with me. I show my ass off to Blue. I can hear him growl, being the only one I haven't tasted yet, I tease him a little more. I wiggle my ass before I stand. I pull each foot out, I toss them to the side as well. If you think I'm wearing matching panties and bra, you'd be wrong. Why would I be? I didn't expect to be hunted down. My thong is appropriate for the day, orange with bats.

"Mmm, these are hot." Red runs his hand over the seam of my thong, pulling the front upwards. I hiss with the added pressure to my clit. He lands a smack to my sensitive clit. I jolt from the bite.

"Oh, fuck. Yes." My knees wobble. I've never had my pussy smacked before. Holy hell does it feel amazing. I can feel wetness on the inside of my thigh, I'm aching for more. Red peels my thong off, revealing my naked pussy in front of him.

With a deep inhale, his finger traces my slit. "Feels amazing, doesn't it." Then he spreads my lips open pinching my clit.

"Fuck." I gasped. The other two step up to my side, my hands dart for their cocks. Giving me something to hold on while I'm thrown into pure ecstasy. Red flicks my clit with his tongue, before he goes back to rubbing it, causing my hips to jerk forwards. He takes hold of my left ankle, lifting my leg up placing it over his shoulder. The other two steady me around the waist. This new position opens me up further. I throw my head back moaning louder. I pump each cock faster the closer I get to my orgasm. As he slips a finger inside, within seconds, he tickles my g-spot. I scream out my orgasm. I move my body back, when I feel liquid squirt out of me.

"That was fucking hot. Let's do that again."

"What the fuck just happened?" I look down at him in horror.

"Baby, you squirted all over him," Green sounds excited when he tells me.

"S-Squirted? It felt like I peed all over him." I try to bring my leg down, but Red only tightens his hold.

He runs his hands up my inner thigh. "That's right, you've never experienced that before. Felt amazing, didn't it?"

I can't explain it, it was overwhelming. My entire body felt like it was on fire. My legs still shaking from the aftershocks. "I've never had it happen before. It's so embarrassing." I fold my head into my hands.

"It's beautiful. I think she's ready for us. Where's the blindfold?"

At the mention of a blindfold, I lift my head. That's adding so much trust in these men, can I do this? Fingers grasp my chin turning my head to face Blue.

"Use your safe word. We already know your hard limits. Anything we do we'll explain, and you can tell us to stop. You understand?" I wish I could see his eyes to see if he was telling me the truth, all I have to go off is his muffled voice. My gut is giving me a small warning, but no huge red flags.

"Okay. Yes. I trust you all."

Electricity intensifies in the air. Sealing my fate for the night. Green walks towards me holding a black silk blindfold. Running his hands over it, my heart jumps when he stands behind me, placing it over my eyes. My world becomes dark. I only have my four senses to go on now. Touch, smell, taste and my hearing. Thankful that they won't take my touch away again.

A hand touches my neck, causing me to jump. Goosebumps trickle over my body when the hand moves alongside my arm. Another hand runs up my thigh, while the last set unclasps my bra. The straps fall before someone removes it fully.

"Oh, fuck. Baby, look at these beauties." I know that's Green from his nickname he uses. When his warm mouth latches onto my nipple, I now realize why I needed the blindfold. They've taken their masks off. He bites on my right nipple, while a hand plays with my clit. The moans slip freely from me now.

A tongue darts out and traces over my clit before sucking it.

"Yes, more, please." My entire body is on fire, it needs something more. A finger is added to my needy core, while he continues to suck my clit. My hand darts out to grip their hair, pushing him further into me.

"Want something else to hold, Wednesday?"

I can only nod. A hand takes hold of the one I'm gripping the hair with, guiding it to the side. When I touch a velvet like tip, I open my hand. There's no piercing, so I know this is Green. A hand threads into my hair turning my head to the side.

"Open for me. I need to feel you." The sound of his voice makes me clench around Red's finger.

"She loves when you talk, I can feel her tighten," Red groaned.

I open for Blue while he slides his cock into my mouth. I take my other hand wrapping it around him. I flick my tongue over his piercing, lowering my head further. When Red hits my g-spot again, I moan around Blue's cock and pump Green faster.

"I'm gonna come if we don't do something soon." Green halts my move, causing me to release him from my grip. Red removes his finger, then Blue pulls out of my mouth.

My chin is tilted upwards, I can feel warm air on either side of my neck. Eventually they kiss down my neck, the sound of foil being torn open, causes my heart to flutter. I can't believe I'm going to have sex with three men. How insane is this?

"Walk forward, he's waiting for you on the couch." With the help of both men, they lead me to the couch where Red is waiting for me. Hands wrap around my waist when I reach him, he has no problem lifting me upwards. I place my hands on his shoulders. He's so broad he could be a football player.

He lines himself up, he already feels too big. "You ready? What's the safe words?"

"Yellow and Red." I barely had the words out of my mouth before he slams me down on him. I let out a scream when he stretched me wide. I can already feel myself coming. A smack is landed on my ass, it startles me at first, then he smacks me again. I groan with hunger. He smacks me one more time, I explode. I grind my hips chasing my orgasm more, digging my fingernails into his shoulders. All while he pounds deeper.

"Don't stop... feels too good." I squeeze my eyes when he groans and grunts. I clench around his throbbing cock.

"Fuck, you feel so good." He palms my breasts, pinching my nipples. "I'm gonna come soon." He grunts out. Next thing I know I'm pulled off him. I hear the condom being ripped off. "Open now." I open my mouth for him right as he comes down my throat. "Yes, I love seeing my cum in your mouth. Stick your tongue out, let me see it all."

I show him what he wants to see, then I swallow it all.

"Good girl, ready for more?"

"Yes, please." I squeeze my thighs together trying to relive some pressure.

I'm lifted onto another body, my hands land on a set of thighs. His large hands glide up my thighs all the way towards my aching pussy. Flicking my sensitive bud, my hips jerk forwards.

"Please, I need you inside of me."

He lets out a chuckle. "You don't even know which one I am." From his voice alone I know it's Green. Blue's voice is deeper and holds more power than the others. Red's voice is Gruff, then Green here his voice is too smooth. Especially with the nickname he gave me. Not that I'll ever let them know I can tell the difference.

I moan when he adds pressure to my clit. My lower stomach begins to cramp with an oncoming orgasm. I'm about to come, when he pulls away. I let out a whimper.

"Don't worry, I've got you." He goes back to rubbing, bringing me closer once again. Only for him to stop.

I let out a small cry. "Oh, God. Don't stop." I'm frustrated all to hell.

"So needy aren't we." He lifts me up, sliding his hard cock inside of me. "Fuck, that feels good. Doesn't it. He warmed you up nicely for me," he groans from behind me. "Use me baby," he said in a choked voice.

I rocked my hips forward, his cock hitting my g-spot every time. A hand touches my cheek.

"You're doing so well. Let's see what else you can do." Blue's pierced cock touches my lips, I dart my tongue out licking the pre-cum from him. His hands thread into my hair pulling it into one hand. The other hand runs down the length of my neck. I swallow deeply when he closes around my neck. "Make me come, with your mouth."

I open for him; he rams his cock all the way in until I gag. While I rock my hips on Green, Blue fucks my mouth. Green pulls my hips back while he takes over, sweat drips down my back from how hard he's working me. All while Blue still rocking in and out of my mouth. Drool falls between my lips all down my breasts. When he finally pulls out, letting me breath deep. Before sliding back in. Groaning when I swallow around him. He thrusts deeper each time Green thrust deep, with one final thrust he comes down my throat. He stays put until I swallow, then pulls out.

"Beautiful. You did real good." He wipes my lips, releasing my hair.

Green thrusts faster, when my orgasm hits me hard. Milking his orgasm from him as well.

"Oh, holy shit," he moaned, going still with one last thrust, he relaxes.

My entire body is spent. I've never had this much pleasure in my life, I'm riding on a high and I never want to get off. Warm arms wrap around my body cradling me into them.

"You did so good. How do you feel?"

"Mmm, like I can sleep for days. My entire body feels like jello."

A kiss lands on my shoulder. "Come, I'll take you upstairs. You can rest."

Even behind the blindfold, my eyes close. I have little energy left in me to care where I go, or how I get there. Even though I should. This night is one that I'll never forget.

I'm placed on a soft surface, fingers brush under the blindfold lifting it off my face. I turn onto my side, slipping further into darkness.

"Think she'll be pissed once she finds out that it's us?"

"Oh, probably. It'll be interesting when she does."

"Be prepared for tomorrow, then. Head to bed, get ready for a battle."

Whatever they are talking about I couldn't be bothered to be worried about. They probably have girlfriends out there that will find out. Not my problem.

I need sleep and lots of it.

4

CATALINA

My body is sore, but in a good way. I've never been railed by three men; well, I guess technically two. Never in my wildest dreams did I ever see this happening. The scary thing is they all seemed somewhat familiar, like I've known them from somewhere before. Especially Green. I swear I've heard his voice daily, but that can't be right. *Can it?* I've must've gotten too much cock last night. That's all.

Cracking open my eyes, I can see where I am. The room I'm in is too bright and cheery for me. The bedding is white; the furniture is white. Why does everything have to be white? The downstairs is perfect. Dark. This room doesn't belong here. I sit up for it to be worse. I swear my grandmother heaved her decor in here. There is a motherfucking afghan draped across the end of the bed. Knitted in different coloured squares. Then on the nightstand is a crochet doily. *Who are these people?* I need to get out of here, and quick.

I find my clothes neatly folded on the dresser. All what's missing are the keys to the van. *Perfect.* Pulling on my leggings, I hear the floorboards creak outside my door. I pause my movements. When the footsteps continue, I quickly finish getting dressed. Peeking through the keyhole on the door, I can't see anything, cracking the door open, it sends out a small groan in protest. *Swing it fast, stupid.* Swinging it fast, it's quieter. Stupid brain always being right. The hallway is empty when I step out. It's decorated in modern Victorian. Burgundy walls, floral floor runner, gold picture frames. It takes my breath away. Heading down the staircase, I take notice of the pictures on the wall. It's filled with frames, not just any frames. There are bats pinned in one, a larger frame with three moths. The oddities only continue the further you go down the stairs. The double-headed mini skull, would be my favourite.

If I were van keys, where would I be? I walk in the direction of the room we were in last night. Maybe Blue left them in there somewhere. Entering the room, I finally get a look at it. It turns out to be a den. A leather couch is angled in front of a fireplace with two accent chairs to the side, still don't know how I didn't notice it yesterday. Bookshelves line the furthest wall, filled to the brim. A small bar cart tucked to the side that's fully stocked. This room reeks like masculinity.

As I look around, I'm remembering what happened from last night. Heat creeps up my neck with the thought of all three of them touching me, I touch my cold hands to my cheeks to cool them down a little. Leaving this room, I hunt down a different room. Maybe the kitchen. This is why, I should always hide an extra set in the fucking gas cap. I've could've snuck out already. I was expecting the kitchen to be empty when I walk in, but it isn't.

Someone is standing at the stove.

Without their shirt on.

Without their mask on.

I'm not sure which one it is between Green or Blue. But sweet baby Jesus, the back muscle. Red is broader, so I know it's not him. But whoever this is. Fuck me again, please. How did I get so lucky for them to find me?

"Oh, sorry. I didn't mean to interrupt. I need my keys. I should be getting back home."

He hummed in return. Not sure what that means, is that a 'okay, sure see ya' or a 'no, you need to stay longer' hum?

He continues going about his business, ignoring me. Not sure what I should do, so I back out of the kitchen. I can tell when I'm usually not wanted. Obviously, we aren't a morning person. I'll try the living room. If they aren't in there, I'll walk home. I'll ask the professor to tow the van at my expense. Even though I can't afford it, I can't leave it sitting here. It's too valuable.

The living room is still quiet when I enter, the only thing is there is now two shirtless men standing by the front window. I gotta swallow the drool that pools in my mouth. One is Red for sure. I wasn't lying when I said he could be a football player.

"Have either of you seen my keys?" I'm starting to get nervous how no one will talk to me. Footsteps fall behind me.

"Wednesday, it's been a real pleasure having you all night."

At the sound of Blue's voice, I turn around.

My world tilts on its axle, my entire life can be seen crashing before my eyes. Atomic bombs have nothing going on with what's happening right now. How did my brain not figure this out before now.

No, no, this can't be happening. I swing my head back around again. My skin crawls, my stomach churns. Bit by bit, I back away from all three of my bullies. Dorian, Nyx and Cole. Tears fill my eyes when last night plays in my mind. I had sex with two of them. I gave all of them blowjobs. My lips tremble, I bring my hand to my mouth, shaking my head.

"This can't be happening. You knew this entire time." My voice cracks at the end.

Dorian steps closer to me. His broad shoulders overshadowing me. "We did. Thanks for last night, by the way."

"We knew you enjoyed it; it's a shame you didn't know our names to scream them." Nyx's smooth voice washes over me.

Turning back to stare at Cole, his blue eyes darkening more. "Don't get us wrong, we enjoyed every sound you made." He tosses something to me. When I catch it, I see it my keys.

"I hate you all!" I scream savagely. "I can't believe you did this to me, this is an all-time low, even for you Cole." I storm towards the front door to the sounds of their laughter.

I've never wanted to die more than I do right now.

I couldn't get the van started fast enough, peeling out of that driveway should've felt refreshing, shame that's what it feels like. I feel like a dirty, worthless person. How could I do this? I should've said no, the first chance I had. Then again, would it really matter. For some unknown reason, they hate me. I drive back to the cemetery. I still have a job to finish even if I want to crawl under the body that I need to bring back. I brush away the tears that continue to fall.

This is such bullshit.

They don't deserve my tears.

No one does.

With that, I pull up my big girl panties, and hopefully try to move on. I can only hope come Monday at school they won't try anything. I can only hope I'll be that lucky. Every day they pull something on me.

Having Nyx in my philosophy class is bad enough, I can't escape him. He sits directly behind me, not rows back or a couple seats to the left. Directly behind me, breathing down my back. Watching my every move, I can't escape him until the class ends. Even then he walks out when I do, then Dorian and Cole meet up with him in the hallway, following close behind me. The last time they did anything was right before Halloween. I should've seen this coming.

Professor Adams kept talking but, I couldn't focus any longer. My night was a little longer than I hoped for. I was gearing up for Halloween night, I knew it was going to be a fucking shit show. When he finally dismissed us, the hairs on the back of my neck raised before I can get out of my seat. I grab my bag, ignoring the dirty looks coming from Nyx. Walking past him, he sticks his foot out tripping me before I can dodge it. Landing on my knees, my bag spills everywhere. Books, tampons, pens. Fucking everything spilled across the floor. Everyone that's left behind laughed. Heat blossomed across my cheeks.

"Oops, my bad. Better luck next time." He lets out a low chuckle before he walks away.

I watch him walk out, meeting up with his buddies. I try to avoid their presence when I finally leave the room. I can hear their mumbles behind me when I try to get more distance between us, if only that lasted.

"What's the matter? Cat got your tongue?" Dorian's voice was closer than I expected.

I keep walking praying they'll leave me be.

"You know, we'll always find you. You'll never be able to escape us, Catalina." The way my name slides out of Cole's mouth sent shivers down my spine.

Cole is the worst of them all. He's ruthless. He's the one that started tormenting me every chance he got. When he couldn't he would send Dorian and Nyx to do the job. Like today, it's up to Nyx to embarrass me, maybe one day I'll figure out what I did to cause all of their attention, but I know for one thing I don't fucking want it.

Life would've been perfect if it wasn't for them. Now I feel like my entire life is a mess, even going to work feels like a form of violation. I look down at the open grave, the body is exactly how I left it. All my equipment thrown around from my quick getaway. The early morning brought in a low coverage of fog, so if I'm going to do this, I better work like a speeding bullet. The last thing I need is a nosy Nancy calling the cops on me. After reapplying the hook to the body, I haul it upwards. The tarp is wet with dew, but it'll have to work. I won't have time for the other one until tonight.

As always, the campus parking lot is empty, same can be said about my soul right now. I'm running on fumes. I only want to get home to wash away the terrible night. After leaving the body, I make sure to restock the van, having everything ready for tonight. Grabbing my keys from the cup holder I head towards my baby. At least driving in her will boost my spirits for a little while. *Hopefully.*

The purr that comes off her is a welcoming sound. Even though she may be a little old for some, she has never disappointed me, like almost everything else in my life I can count on her. Johnny has gotten me out of some terrible times, moved me to this fucked up town and after graduation she'll be moving me again. I don't know what I would do without her. While driving back to my apartment, I can see all the destruction that went on last night. Litter lines the road, driving past the park. I can see people passed out in compromised positions. So disgusting. That's where the kids fucking play you pigs. Now your cock and balls have literally touched all the playground equipment. I want to throw up, this town it drives me mad. You are all probably asking yourselves. 'Then why did you move here, Cat?' I'll tell you. The art program at EU is the best, also doesn't help that I won a scholarship, so I don't have to pay back so many student loans. If I knew what I was getting myself into with the three men and this backwards of a town, I would have gone to a smaller school. Not that I have any family waiting for me or any I give a shit about anymore. The joys of writing them all off. I don't need drama. I like to avoid it any chance I can. Then what happens. Dorian Prescott, Nyx Thornton, and Cole Valentine, stupid last name if you ask me, he isn't filled with love his heart is filled with darkness.

The second I unlock my door, I can feel the stress leave my body. One step closer to that bed, which has been calling my name for hours, I'm a dirty fucking mess. I still need to clean the cut on my head from the tombstone yesterday. You would think that they would've fixed me up a little before they had their fun, but apparently all they were thinking about was getting off. I can't say much, I was too. I'll never forgive myself for what I did.

"That's because you're stupid Cat."

I flick on the light in the bathroom, finally looking at myself in the mirror. I flinch when I see my forehead. The gash is bigger than I expected. I'm surprised I didn't have a headache from it. Opening the cabinet, I dig around until I find a washcloth, I don't have a first aid kit, it'll have to go unbandaged.

After I clean it, I climb into the shower. Washing away all the filth until my skin turns pink. My mind keeps flashing back to last night after they all took me to their house, I should've known something was wrong, yet my gut never warned me, unless you count the white bandana from Nyx's back pocket. That should've been a clue to who they were.

I wanted it.

How sad is that?

Is my life so pathetic that I wanted a little action and adventure, that I was willing for strangers at the time to take me. Then the second I find out it's the three of them, I run instead of facing them and telling them how I really feel about them and giving them hell.

Loser, that's what I am. That's what I'll always be.

5

COLE

This morning was a whirlwind, after Catalina left, I received a phone call from the president of our gang. Telling us to get our asses down to the warehouse. I didn't bother asking questions, I knew better. Belonging to the Soul Stealers, we had important roles to play. We're all enforcers so if he's calling its gotta be important, no matter how much I want to relive Cat's mouth in my mind, we have to head out.

"This better be good. I have important shit to do today," Dorian grumbled as he pulled his pants on.

"*Seriously?* I highly doubt he would be calling us for a spot of fucking tea," Nyx called from his bedroom.

I sometimes question how I'm still friends with these two. Even after all these years, we've stuck together. We've seen some weird shit, been through the worst and yet stayed together. I have a feeling whatever we're about to get into today won't be anything different. After last night, this town is going to be a mess. After the new mayor took over, he had new ideas he wanted to try. One being no rules on Halloween night. I think it was a way for him to experiment without being called out on it, fucking pig if you ask me. Now we're responsible to clean up his mess.

"Hey, I need a lift to my bike." I call to no one in particular. I hated to leave it last night, but I'm sure it was safe in the cemetery. Not many people went there, I'll admit I was a little surprised to see *her* there, we were only kidding when we said we were watching her. We were only doing a drive by when I noticed a van parked there. I figured it was another drug van. When we saw it was her, we came up with our plan.

"I can give you a lift, you're riding bitch though." Dorian pats me on the back before walking down the stairs. Fuckin' prick.

I throw on my hoodie as I jog downstairs. The guys are waiting for me like always, I'm not sure how I became the leader of this group of ours, but it seems fitting Dorian brings the muscles, Nyx is the calm one of the group. Me, I'm the cruel one. I take no pity on anyone. I could give two shits on how they feel, think anyone cares about my feelings? The answer you're searching for is no. So, the faster you learn that the world is a cesspool the quicker we'll get along.

The first day of November is always chilly, but thankful enough we never have to give up riding our bikes. If I ever had to move to a snowy location, that's the day I'll visit the cemetery for good.

Dorian rides like a fucking pussy, the quicker I can feel the vibration of my own bike the better. Eastwood Cemetery is in the middle of town. Rather weird to build a town around dead people, then they have another cemetery because one wasn't enough. I'm telling you, this town is weird. Yet, people still move here. When the cemetery comes into view, I feel relieved when I see that my bike is still parked where we left it, *thank God.* I pity anyone that would've touched her. I look around for anything that belongs to her, but you couldn't even tell she was here. I have so many questions about what the fuck we witnessed.

"We better hurry before Henry loses his fucking gasket," Nyx said, gripping his handlebars of his black Harley Davidson Street Bob. Well, to be honest we all have Street Bob's. Mine's grey, and Dorians is red. It's the best for quick getaways, when you do what we do, you need to be quick.

"Yeah, yeah. He won't say anything until we get there, anyway. He can hold his fuckin' pants for all I care," I say as I climb on my beauty. Tilting my head, they follow when I take off. The ride to the warehouse is calming to my soul. The town is a disaster. If this is the reason Henry is calling, it'll be for a clean-up, as much as I love taking part in the Halloween festivities. Clean up duty is the least part of the fun. When Henry agreed to this with the mayor, I don't think this is what he had in mind. But it keeps everyone off our backs.

Our warehouse is at the edge of town, surrounded by trees. If you didn't know what you were looking for, you would miss it from the road. The Soul Stealers' residence is one of a kind. The warehouse houses the office, gun room and my favourite room. The torture room. I could eat and sleep in it. Every time a body is brought to my door, I'm ready to get answers from them. Whatever it takes, I'm down for it. A broken bone here, a stab wound there. Hell, I even go as far as shoving a metal rod up one dude's dick before. He squealed like a fuckin' pig with all the secrets we were waiting for. Men are easy to get answers from. They really value their dicks.

Behind the warehouse, is a few empty sheds. Henry tried to convert them into houses, but no one wanted to stay in them. We all felt like it threw off cultic vibes. So, we have our own places in town instead. Which works well considering we all go to school. Something I wish we didn't have to do. It's Henry's wishes everyone in the gang must attend university. I think it's the most half-witted idea he's ever had. Like what gang member is educated? Luckily, it's only one more year and I'm fuckin' finished. With a useless degree that I'll never use.

"Come on, let's get this over with. I'm sure it has something to do with the mess the town is in."

"Oh, one hundred percent. Did you see the park? All those naked bodies. I only have one stuck in my head that I won't be getting out of my mind anytime soon," Dorian groaned, while adjusting himself.

I can hear Nyx groan behind me as well. "I'd have to agree. She was amazing. I still think we could've gone a different way this morning."

I stop dead in my tracks turning around. "Seriously. That's what you're worried about? I didn't hear you complain when you were balls deep in that cunt of hers."

He throws his hands up. "Hey man, that's not what I meant, and you know it. All I'm saying is we could've done things differently."

See the thing with Nyx is, although he's the calm one. He's also the nicest one. He hates when we need to teach Catalina a lesson. The reasons aren't important right now.

I head towards the warehouse door, not waiting for them. Pushing the door open I'm greeted with everyone that's in the gang. Freddy sitting by the office door keeping watch of who's coming and going. He's got to be pushing ninety, but I've seen him kill a guy just last week. He's not one to mess with. He's also lived in this town his entire life, so he's the one to ask about anything. The boys and I usually meet up with him on Sundays for coffee and small talk. It's nice to have someone older to have a decent conversation with. He waves us into the office with a dip of his chin. I dip my head in return before I find my seat at the large table.

Now you might think this is like a MC club, but no. We are far from that. We are worse, we're a gang. We aren't called Soul Stealers for a reason. The only rank this gang has is technically Henry. The only reason we are called the enforcers are because we aren't afraid to finish a fuckin' job. We deal in drugs, guns, prostitutes and more. When I say we are worse, trust me on this. We don't deal with a sexual Halloween purge for nothing.

Henry clears his throat before he talks. "All right girls, some things have been happening around town that no one can explain." He looks around at every single one of us. Pausing dramatically. I can't help but roll my eyes.

"Spill it Henry, it can't be that exciting," I tell him, trying to hold back a yawn.

"Always with the negativity, aren't you, Cole. If you must know. Someone has been playing around in our backyard. There is apparently a new dealer in town. I need to send them a little message. Give them the royal treatment, if you know what I mean. I'm sending Cole and his boys out on this one." He nods at me, I keep a straight face showing no emotion. I can't let him know how much I'm looking forward to this. After last night, I need more of an outlet. Don't get me wrong, coming down Catalina's throat was amazing, but I need the real thing from her.

"On it, you won't be disappointed."

He gives me a smirk. "Never am with you. I'll text the details to your burner."

With that, he dismisses us. Whoever this new dealer is, he's in for a real treat, that's for sure. I don't put up with new meat very well, especially ones that take food from our own mouths. This town isn't big enough for more than one dealer. Surprisingly enough, it's big enough for a university but that thing is older than time. Most of the outbuildings should be condemned. It's disgusting how far this town has let the buildings go to waste, they only care about the medical buildings. It's what brings the most students here, not that I'll complain they are our biggest drug clients.

"So, what's the plan? Go in like always and ruff them up a little?" Nyx questioned as we walk outside.

"Nah, I have a better idea. Dorian, do you still have those explosive packs we used last time?"

"Like you have to fuckin' ask," he says with a slight laugh. "How many packs do you think you need? Anything else?"

"Maybe a three and a couple of timers. We'll drop by, say our peace, then blow up their shit to really seal the deal. If that doesn't tell them we're serious, then they really are dense."

They both laugh, but I know they are excited for tonight. Killing gets us all amped up. The only thing that would be better, is a nice warm pussy to sink our dicks into. I have to stop thinking of Catalina so much, it's only pissing me off even more. I just didn't think she would respond to us the way she did. Even if she didn't know who we were at the time. She handed over all control. I didn't think she would, my dick twitches with the thought of her under my control again. With that thought, I start my bike taking off back to the house. I can't let her get under my skin, it was one thing to let her suck me off, but it's another thing to keep thinking about her.

The streets are a little cleaner, another thing about the mayor. His image is everything. If word got around what this town did, other mayors would be ashamed of him. The only saving grace is they hold a meeting here every year mid November. So, he has no choice but to clean the town up. If any major riots did break out, he would have so much explaining to do. I almost want to cause one next year just to watch him piss his pants in front of everyone. By the time we roll into the driveway, I'm already thinking of ways of destroying our competition. Let me tell you it'll be sweet, sweet revenge when I'm finished with them.

When it's time to go, we load our bikes. When I look over at Dorian. He's all smiles when he loads his side saddles with his bag of goodies. You be surprised to learn that he isn't taking chemistry in school. He's only taking what he needs to for a shitty degree that he won't be using. His life is the gang and only the gang. Nyx, on the other hand is harder to read, his face is nothing but his poker face. He'll keep everything inside until the last second. Don't think because he speaks softly that he won't blow your brains out. That's how he draws his enemies closer.

It's late evening by the time we roll into the South-side of town. I have to laugh at the name they call themselves. Death Eaters. Like fucking come on. It's like they placed names in a hat and that's the one they pulled out. I swear someone in that gang likes *Harry Potter* too much. Their house isn't anything to get excited about. It sits in the middle of two other houses. One house is abandoned and boarded up. The other looks to be occupied. I'm not one for innocent casualties, but I can't risk a gang member living in that house if we tell them to leave.

Dorian must be on the same page as I am. "I'm going to set the explosive on the left side, so the abandoned house takes the most abuse."

"I would agree. I'll keep watch. I'll send the signal if I see anything," I tell him before he creeps towards the side of the house.

Nyx scans the area, while I keep watch on the gang's house. The only sound is the thumping of bass coming out of the house. Sounds like they are having a grand old time. Too bad we're about to crash it like a bunch of pricks that we are.

Dorian comes running back giving us a thumbs up. "I'll blow them once we leave, I set them around the back close to the basement. I'm sure that's where they set up production."

"Good, let's head in."

For a drug house, it was kept clean outside. I guess they really didn't want the cops to be showing up at their doorstep anytime soon. They should've thought on us instead. Drawing our guns, I didn't even bother knocking. I give Dorian a nod, with one swift kick the door crashes down. The music stops instantly. We are greeted with guns pointed at our faces. I couldn't help but laugh.

"Seriously." I spread my arms out wide. "You all have the balls. Who's in charge here?" Looking around, I wait for someone to point out the asshole I'm about to destroy. When no one makes a move, I cock my desert eagle and shoot the nearest person. The thud when the body hit the floor sends a flurry all around us.

Three against, well to be honest I couldn't even count them all. It doesn't matter, cause Nyx is dropping them like flies. He's the only one that can double-fist his desert eagles, firing a path on either side of him, looking like a total badass. Which don't get me wrong, he really is. He may be the shortest between the three of us, but he's a killing machine. I'm still trying to find the fucking leader. Henry gave me a brief description of him, shave head, short. Like, what kind of description is that? Anyone is short compared to my six-foot frame. Like is he skinny like a twig, got a belly? Old or young. Nah nothing like that. I could've shot the fuck by now.

"Where's your leader?" I grip some cunt by his shirt.

He spits on my hoodie. "I ain't tellin' you shit."

I look down at his gob of spit, curling my lip I look back at him. "Either you tell me, or I'll place a bullet in your dick, and you'll never be able to use it on a pussy again."

He pales placing his hands over his dick. "He's in the basement."

"His name."

"S... Spencer, his name is Spencer," he stumbled out.

I shoot him anyway. I'm not a nice person re-member. He howls in pain. I only smile at his pain. "Thanks, sorry about your dick. My finger slipped."

I whistle for the boys. Letting them know where I'm headed. If you thought I would stick around for a fight, I'm about to start a new one. Apparently, with a guy named Spencer, I trust the boys to deliver a good message from me. The basement is well-lit with tables lined the entire length. Weed and Coke laid out waiting to be delivered. There's a room in the back which I'm going to guess Spencer is hiding like a little bitch.

"Spencer, come out, come out wherever you are," I sang out, making my way towards the room I know he's in. I hear a crash inside. Not very quiet now, is he? Twisting the doorknob, I fling it open so fast I catch him trying to climb out the window. He slips landing on the cement floor on his back.

"Oh, Spence. That's not how this is going to work. You see. I heard from a certain bird called the Soul Stealers that you decided to sell drugs in our town. That's not going to work for us."

He lets out a small whimper. "I swear I didn't know. I thought it was free game."

"See, now we both know that's bullshit. Eastwood is known for their gang. It's in your best interest to pack up and move out before something else happens. Compeesh?" I stand over him hovering my foot over his hand, waiting for him to answer. When he hesitates. I step down. Crunching his fingers under the weight of my foot.

He screams, struggling to remove his hand. "I asked if you under-fuckin-stood. This isn't going to be an all-night conversation, so answer me."

"Yes! I get it. I'll leave," he yelled, while still struggling.

I lift my foot; he cradles his hand into his chest. "I also advise you to haul your ass upstairs and call your dirty men off mine. If they aren't dead by now."

Upstairs is nothing but a bloodbath. Everything is covered in red. With a shout from Spencer, his men halt their fighting. Perfect timing because I need this night to end. I'm sure Dorian is waiting to send them his big boom.

"Fuck this, let's go. He was dealt with. If he can't figure out we're serious, that's on him."

"Good. I have some schoolwork to finish," Nyx informs us as we make our way outside.

"You always have some form of work to do. I don't know why you even try," Dorian grunted.

"It's because I don't want to be stuck in a gang for my entire life, Dorian," he spat out.

"Okay, that's enough. Fight at home." I cut in before they get too far into a fight and we forget our actual purpose.

"Whatever. The timer will go off in five." He storms off towards his bike.

Work with your friends they say, it'll be fun they say. It's a fuckin' headache.

A huge boom is heard. I look back and the side of the house was gone. A huge fireball is shot up to the sky lighting up the neighbourhood. You can feel the heat from where we're parked at the end of the street. I'm pretty sure we delivered our message loud and clear. Don't be doing business in our town. You won't be surviving.

By the time we get home, we're all beat.

"I'm calling it a night. I'll see you guys tomorrow." I wave at them before heading upstairs. I need to wash the night off. I can tell you one thing, I'm not looking forward to going to school tomorrow. Okay, that's a lie.

I'm looking forward to fucking with my Wednesday.

6

NYX

I was never the one for school. I hated it especially in high school. The only thing that keeps me going now is a certain raven-haired woman that sits in front of me in Philosophy. Yes, that may seem weird to some, but Catalina really is a beauty. Ever since the day I walked in here, I was blown away. Then Cole made me watch every move she made, whatever she did to him that day really set him off.

I can't complain, except I can't handle hurting her anymore. I can tell by the way her body stiffens that she knows I'm watching her. I'm sure she's waiting for us to pull another stunt like we did Halloween night. To be honest, I really want a repeat of that night, but getting her to that point again I don't see happening now that she knows it was us.

She turns her head ever so slightly catching me watching her. Her eyes are what draws me in the most. I've never met anyone with violet eyes before. It wasn't hard to figure out who she was in the cemetery. I never take my eyes off her, we continue to stare that is until Professor Adams' voice cuts between us.

"Mr. Thornton, is Miss. Wilson more entertaining than I am?"

Catalina swings her head to the front; I can't help but smirk at her. "Sorry professor couldn't help myself. You know how it is when a beautiful girl is around, all logical things are tossed out the window."

"Yes, well, not in my class or next time the both of you will stay behind."

Her head snaps upwards. I'm pretty sure she wanted to say something, but she never got a chance. Professor Adams got back to teaching the class about theoretical philosophy. I still never paid attention; I went back to watching Cat. By the time we were dismissed, I came up with a plan. One that doesn't involve the other two. I watch her gather her bag, when she stands I damn near came in my pants. She's wearing black knee-high socks held up by a garter, a black miniskirt with chains hanging off her belt. Her graphic t-shirt is hidden under a leather jacket. Only she could make all that black look sexy. I have to hold back the groan when she locks eyes with me again. She looks nervous when she steps out of her row, I let her get to the door before I follow.

"Hey, Catalina, wait up," I call out to her.

She doesn't bother slowing down or looking back. She picks up the pace trying to add distance between us. That's fine, I don't mind the chase.

"Catalina, please. I only want to talk."

"Get away from me, Nyx. I don't have anything I want to say to you." She turns down a hallway that's almost vacant. Wrong move, baby.

Her stride is smaller than mine and I have no problem catching up to her. I grab her by the elbow, dragging her into an empty room.

"Let go of me." She wiggles in my grip; I only tighten my hold on her.

"You're not going anywhere, baby."

"Don't fuckin' call me that you pig. What you guys did to me was wrong."

I laugh. "Really, because from where I was standing you were begging for all of us, you said the words *yes*."

She glares up at me. I spin her around holding her back to my chest. Pinning her arms to her sides. Her chest rises rapidly, pushing her breasts out every time. I couldn't help myself. I lower my face into her nape. I breathe deep. She smells like apples and honey.

"You smell so good, baby." I kiss her neck upwards her ear. "Wanna play a little game? Just you and me?" I can feel her body slowly melt into mine.

"Not really. I don't fully trust you. How do I know this isn't some sort of trap?"

I bite her earlobe, sliding my hand away from her wrist. "You'll have to trust me." I continue sliding my hand until I reach the hem of her skirt. She doesn't stop me when I run my finger under feeling her smooth skin of her thigh. "Yes, or no?"

Her breath hitches when I slide higher, I run my other hand over her stomach pushing her into my hard-on. I run my finger back and forth waiting for an answer, slowly inching closer to her panties. I can tell she's holding back.

"Baby, I can feel your heat, but I'm dying to sink my finger inside of you. Don't you miss how Dorian made you feel?" I place kisses along her jaw, getting a moan out of her. "Yes, baby, I love when you make that sound. Do you feel what you do to me." I push her ass into me more, groaning when she rotates her hips. "Fuck me, that's it. Give me a yes." After a long pause, she finally answers.

"Yes, Nyx make me feel good." Turning her body, she looks into my eyes, I can see she doesn't fully trust me. Maybe with time she will. I only need to convince Cole and Dorian to give up their bullying. I cup her face; she flicks her gaze to my lips for a second. That's all the welcoming I need. I slam my lips to hers. Her lips are soft against mine, I nip her lower lip before I lift her up with one hand. Her hands wrap around my neck pulling me in deeper. Pinning her to the door, I slip my hand under her skirt moving her thong to the side. She is soaking wet for me.

"So wet for me already, baby." I flick my finger over her clit.

She pulls away. "Nyx," she moaned my name.

"Yeah? You like that?"

I sink a finger deep inside. "Oh, God... I like that a lot."

Her hips rock looking for more, placing another finger in, her core tightens immediately. She's so wet, it's dripping down her thigh. I walk her over to an empty desk. Placing her down on her feet, I spin her around.

"Lean over and hold on."

She's a little hesitant, but listens. I unbutton my jeans, the sound of my zipper her head snaps up.

"W-what are you doing?"

I pull my cock out and start pumping it. Her pupils dilate watching me, licking her lips. She doesn't turn away.

"Turn around baby," I groaned.

With one final look, she lays back down. I lift her skirt up, sliding her thong down her thighs. Her wet pussy glistening in the light. I pump faster when I sink my fingers back inside of her. Pulling out I wipe her juices on my cock.

"God, you feel amazing on my cock." I run my finger over her tight rosebud. "Have you ever had anyone in here before?"

She shakes her head. I spit on her tight hole, before pushing the tip of my finger inside.

"Holy shit, Nyx," she yelled.

"Yes, scream my name." I run the tip of my cock along her entrance, pushing in slowly watching as her pussy pulls me inside. "You, feel so good, baby." I rock my hips forwards until I'm fully inside, while pumping my finger in her tight ass.

"I'm gonna come."

I can feel her grip me, I groan and rock harder and faster. The desk moves forward scraping along the floor, but neither one of us cares. I'm grab her by the waist with my hand when she screams her release, I pull my finger out of her ass and hold on to her as I move deeper.

"Nyx don't stop. I'm coming again."

As she finds her release, she milks mine from me. It came out of nowhere, leaving me breathless.

"Holy shit, baby." I lean my forehead on her back.

She hums her response. She tilts her head to the side. Her eyes are closed, but she has a smile on her face. "That felt amazing, I've never done anything with my ass before, I was always too scared to try." She glances at me. "Thank you for being so gentle with me. I don't know why you are suddenly."

I shrug, because honestly, I don't know either. "Maybe it's time for a change." I pull out of her tucking myself back into my pants.

"Well, I don't know about Cole. I don't know what I did to him for him to hate me."

I frown. How is that possible? Cole said she knew the reason. I don't understand any of this.

"We better head out before someone walks in, what class do you have next?"

She straightens her skirt, then grabbing her bag. "I have an art class, but I'm sure I missed most of it. Which fuckin' sucks. So, I'll head home for the day."

"I'll walk you out."

"That won't be necessary. I'm sure you have a class to catch or whatever you do." She walks towards the door, leaving before I can say anything.

For the rest of the day, all I could think about was Catalina Wilson. When I get home, Cole is on a rampage. I guess Henry is being a hardass, wanting us to pull extra duty on the town's border to make sure we don't have any other mishaps like we just had. To be honest, he should've caught it sooner, he is the fuckin' leader of the gang and really, it's his job to be scouting the entire town for problems. Yes, I know we're the enforcers. But we only enforce what he tells us to, so if he doesn't say anything we can't take matters into our own hands. We tried that once, when a bunch of frat boys went after a girl. We handled things. Henry lost his shit on us. We never went rogue again. In a way, it's his fault this happened. If he didn't place us on a leash, we would've figured it out before all of this.

Now Cole is yelling at whoever is in his crosshairs. I should've gone for a drive instead of coming home or found Cat. Anything is better than listening to him.

He's also pissed off that he didn't get to pull anything on her today. *Oops, my bad*, guess I kept her from him. I've tried asking him why we keep doing things to her, but he only accuses me of things. I'm better off keeping quiet. He doesn't need to know that Cat is trusting me, all I can do for now is keep Cole off her back and hopefully he'll come around. Maybe it was a misunderstanding. All I know is once something is in his head, good luck getting it out. He has a way of twisting the truth to his liking.

I need a plan for him to see what I see in her. I wonder if I can think of something that will force them together somehow.

7

CATALINA

I can't get what happened with Nyx out of my head. Crazy right. Am I going crazy?

"Bitch you might be." I tell myself. I lied to him. I didn't have a class. I had to head home to prepare for tonight. Turns out I have another job. The dead never rest in this town. Lucky me. I need a clear head for tonight, and having Nyx weasel inside isn't helping. I don't know if I can fully trust his motives especially when he's friends with Cole. Dorian seems like an okay person. The other night he didn't come off like he would hurt me and the next morning he only said one thing to me, although he did come off as an ass beforehand. He's harder to read. He also follows along with what Cole says.

Jesus Cat, get your head in the game and not Nyx's dick game. *Oh, but what a dick he has indeed.*

I swiftly change out of my skirt, and knee-highs throwing on a pair of leggings. The usual uniform for grave robbing I guess, and you guessed it messy bun. You get great at the messy bun when you usually run late. That and I'm horrible at doing any hair style. It was the one thing my mother figure lacked at teaching me. She was more interested in all the sons she produced. Leaving no room for me. When you are wedged in the middle of four boys, you tend to get lost.

That's all I can handle about thinking of her. Dr. Deadbodies wanted to have a talk with me before I head out. I double check that I packed everything, including snacks. Can never forget the snacks or wet wipes oh and hand sanitizer for obvious reasons. Johnny waits for me in my driveway as always, never letting me down. Is it that sad that my car is the only one I can rely on? *Just say no.*

The drive to the school brought back more memories that I didn't want to remember. I knew I shouldn't let my mind wander into my past. I kept that door closed for a reason. My mother and her sons were spiteful people. I couldn't wait to leave that house, whatever Cole throws at me is nothing compared to what I had to deal with in that house. Chills race down my back when I think of the very last time her sons tormented me.

They tied my hands behind my back stuffing me inside the closet of my room. All four of them left me there for two days before coming to check on me. I was so dehydrated I couldn't talk; my lips were cracked and bleeding. That didn't seem to matter to them because they hauled me out by my hair, my screams going unheard. My joints were so sore from sitting in one spot for so long, that my legs didn't want to work but that didn't stop them. I was tossed into the middle of my room; I can still see their evil eyes staring at me. I never asked why they were doing this to me, I had a feeling it was because of Mother. She didn't want a girl; she wanted me gone. I never understood why she never gave me up, or why my dad never stepped in and said something. He stood by while she let her sons do whatever they wanted. But after that night, they beat me so badly; I thought I was going to die. They kicked and punched me all while my hands were tied. I moved out shortly after, finding whatever work I could and bought Johnny. I lived in my car until I graduated high school, then I received my scholarship and moved here.

What a childhood, right? Like I said, I have family just none that I give a shit about.

The campus parking lot has a few cars spread out. It's almost eight, so I'm pretty sure most of these are for the clubs that will be ending soon. Parking in my usual spot I walk towards the medical entrance. Dr. Deadbodies is already waiting for me outside. He flicks his cigarette on the ground before he opens the door.

"You know, professor, those things will kill you."

"Oh, probably. Then you would have the fun time of digging me back up."

"Yeah, pass. No offence, but I ain't touching you when you're dead."

He hums, then passes me. We walk down the hall-way towards his office, it's quiet. The only sound is the clicking of our shoes on the floor. I can't complain. Sometimes the quiet is nice, but with the thoughts running rapid in my head I kinda want some chatter.

"Did I do something wrong? Is that why you wanted to talk?" I ask as soon as we step inside his office.

He doesn't say anything. He simply sits in his seat folding his hands on top of his desk. I readjust my bag setting it on my lap folding my arms over it.

"Want to tell me what happened the other night? I asked for three bodies I received one, then the next day I had another one."

I should've known this would come up, I can't really tell him I got railed by three men now can I. Clearing my throat. "Things didn't go as planned."

He raises his forehead giving me a *no shit* look. "Explain Catalina."

"Right, after the first one I headed into town. Things already became unhinged with Halloween *activities*. When I was digging up the grave, I was interrupted by a bunch of teenagers. I had no choice but to pack it in before I was exposed. I figured that was the safest thing to do."

He continues to stare; I can only hope he believes my lie. He leans back in his chair giving me a nod.

"Let's try not to get caught again. I can't afford to lose bodies. I'm on a tight schedule this year and I need all the ones I can get. I have two for you tonight, think you can handle them?"

I give him a small scoff. "Have I ever come up short before now?"

"No, that's why I was concerned. If you need help, I'm here."

I stand letting him know I'm finished. Fuck if I'm letting him help me when I don't need him. He knows which ones I can't do. I head to the van with anticipation. At least I can get my frustration out tonight. I have no choice but to get both bodies in or who knows what would happen. I've never actually had this happen before. I feel like a major failure. I haven't felt this way since I was living with my mother. When she kept telling me she wished I was a boy, or how she wished I could be more like her sons and less like a slut, that I'll be one when I grow up. Well, I'm not far off, I had sex with three men in one night, so congratulations mother your wish came true.

The cemetery is deserted just the way I like it. I figured I'll start with the body I didn't grab. It's located around the same area as the last one. I really wish I could drive closer. The walk to the grave is quiet, far cry from the other night. No motorcycles revving in the distance, no one yelling or cheering. Just complete silence.

"Excellent working conditions." I let out a deep sigh as my shovel sinks into the ground.

I'm laying the tarp out getting ready to drag the body out when I hear motorcycles in the distance.

"You've got to be kidding me." I grind my teeth. I jump into the pit and hook everything up. Fuck if I'm getting caught again. Why can't I work in peace anymore. Popping my head up I look around making sure the coast is clear, I climb the rest of the way out hauling the body once I'm situated.

I wrap everything up and drive to the next site. I don't see the point of driving back to the school for a drop off when I can do everything at one time. I can still hear the revving of engines. I'm happy that they haven't come any closer to me, lets pray it stays that way.

The next grave is near the far back, I'll admit this part of the cemetery is very eerie. The tombstones are older, some are falling over while some have moss over taking them. If I believed in zombies, this would be the time for one to pop up out of the ground. Shivers race down my spine. Never have I ever felt like this before. Maybe it's some bad mojo going on with this body. That's what I tell myself as I continue to walk deeper and deeper. I see the fresh mound of dirt just up ahead. Relief washes over me. I don't have to get closer to the tree line. It's almost one and I swear that's when the crazies come out. Even after Halloween, they still try to pull things. I don't fully trust the gang that runs this town. If they ever found out what I've been up too, well, I'll be afraid of the outcome.

My muscles are screaming at me to take a break, that's when I realized I should've eaten something before I headed out. Good thing for those snacks. Wiping my hands off I grab a granola bar, I glance around the cemetery taking everything in, that's when I see them walking towards me. I don't have time to run.

"Don't even think about it Wednesday. We see you." Cole's deep voice breaks the silence of the night.

My breathing stops. I've been doing this for over a year, and I've never been busted. Why suddenly are these three showing up here? Disturbing me. For the second time this week.

I lower my granola bar. "What the fuck are you guys doing here?"

"Business, can't say. But this." Cole points to the grave I've been digging. "Looks to be more interesting. Do tell."

"Um, yeah, I don't trust you enough so. No thanks." I go to pack up when a hand is wrapped around my arm.

"This doesn't look good baby." Nyx brushes dirt off my cheek while checking out all my gear.

I lean up on my tiptoes to whisper into his ear. "Still not going to tell you."

Dorian walks forwards giving me a smirk. "I might know a way for her to tell us."

"Oh yeah, do tell pretty boy?"

Nyx grips my waist moving me against his chest, as Dorian moves forwards, running his hands up my waist slowly leading to my breasts. My nipples harden when he squeezes them. My clit throbs and I'm embarrassed how fast I've gotten wet for him.

"That's it baby, let him make you feel good just like I did earlier today," Nyx whispered in my ear. I can only nod, even though I know better, but I can't help it. My body has a mind of its own and I can't control it anymore.

Dorian takes me from Nyx carrying me away. "I need to feel you on my tongue again. I've been thinking of you since that night. You tasted so sweet on my lips. Are you ready?"

Oh fuck. I clench my thighs tighter when he sets me down on the ground. Nyx and Cole watch a few feet away. Looking very interested.

His lips land on my neck, I need to grip his shoulders when my knees grow weak. He walks me backwards until my legs hit something cold and solid.

"Lay backwards, hands over your head." The intense stare he gives me leaves no room for an argument.

I turn to look at what I'm lying on. It's a tombstone. *Holy shit,* this is going to happen in a cemetery of all places. When I'm fully laid down, I place my hands over my head. His warm hands move under my ass pulling my leggings down to my ankles.

"Ankles together and push your knees open. I want to see your wet pussy," he demands.

I do what he says, and he groans.

"Cole, get over here, want to see what you're missing out on."

I tilt my head to see his eyes flare, even in the dark I can see how much he's resenting me. To make matters worse, I bit my lip and moan. I can tell he wants this. Maybe this will help change his mind towards me.

I gasp when Dorian flicks my clit with his tongue. My fingers flex looking for something to grab, my fingers brush against a pair of jeans. Tilting my head upwards, my gaze landed on Coles. I watch as his hands move to his waist unbuttoning his jeans; he moves his hand inside his briefs pulling out his hard cock. His piercing shines under the moonlight. When his thumb moves over the tip spreading his pre-cum around, I turn my eyes back to his. I slide my tongue along my dry lips.

"Make me come," he tells me.

He moves closer spreading his legs wide. Lining his velvety smooth tip against my lips, I open wide for him. He groans when he glides along my tongue. Dorian chooses that moment to plunge two fingers into my wet core. I scream around Cole's cock; he thrusts deeper causing me to gag. His hands move to my breasts squeezing as he fucks my mouth.

"Add a finger to her tight asshole, she loves that." I can hear Nyx tell Dorian. He slides his fingers out of my pussy and rub it around my tight hole.

"Fuck, this is amazing. I can tell you love all of your holes being played with, don't you?" Cole said, breathless while he slows his pace.

Dorian pushes his finger into my ass, I grip Cole's thighs and moan around his cock. My hips tilt looking for more. My clit is throbbing needing release, my entire body is on fire. Cole pumps a few more times before pulling out. He strokes himself.

"Fuck, I want your eyes on me when I come."

Dorian pulls his finger out of me, pulling me upwards. "On your knees for him."

Cole doesn't waste any time plunging his cock back into my mouth, his hand wraps around the back of my neck holding me still. Tears run down my cheeks every time he makes me gag. He hisses when I swallow around him.

"Yes, I'm coming. Hold it all don't swallow until I tell you too." His hips jerk forwards before he stills. Warm cum shoots into my mouth. He slowly pulls out. "Open let me look." I show him, he pushes his two fingers inside my mouth until I gag. "Mmm good girl, swallow."

"Fuck, that was hot. Let me finish what I started." Dorian came up behind me pushing my face into the ground. My ass is exposed to the sky. Cole places his wet fingers against my asshole.

"I'll help you, push some of my cum inside of that beautiful ass." Cole pushes two fingers inside.

"Holy shit!" I scream. Pushing back against him. Fingers rub my sensitive clit bringing my climax on quickly. The pull in my lower stomach is intense. Explosions are all around me. "Oh shit, shit. I'm fuck—" I never did finish my sentence the tremors hit, and I collapse. Thank God for the cool grass under my cheek. I'm on fire.

Then I remember I still have to dig up a fuckin' body.

8

DORIAN

Making Catalina come is like pure heaven. Nothing else compares.

She's currently on the ground reeling in from her intense orgasm. Nyx kneels in front of her brushing her hair away from her face.

"You okay?"

She hums giving him a smile.

"Come on, we best get you back into the human world." He gives her a kiss to her forehead before moving her into his lap. When I glance at Cole, he looks perplexed. I know he has mixed emotions for Cat. I only wish he could let everything go. When I look back at Nyx, he's pulling Cat's legging back up.

"Wanna tell us what you're doing out here now?" Cole asked.

Catalina studies him. "Cole, I still don't know what I did to deserve your bullying. I keep replaying everything over and over ever since I started here. Did I say or do something to you? I need to know." Her eyes are begging for him to tell her.

Nyx and I have been wondering the same thing. We don't enjoy pulling our stunts on her, but pissing Cole off is another level that we don't like crossing, either.

"Fucking tell her already, don't be such an asshole. I'm pretty sure she has a right to know by now. Besides, I'm out, I'm not doing it anymore," I told him. He can figure his own shit out. She isn't some toy to be played with. Besides, I enjoy playing a new game with her.

"Yeah man, I'm with D. She deserves so much more from us." Nyx adds. I had my suspicion that he also wanted out.

Cole glares at us. "Why am I getting ganged up on suddenly? I bully her because she's fucking her professor."

My head snaps towards Cat. Her eyes shoot open. Nyx looks at her with disgust.

"W-What the hell. I've never done anything like that. Why would you say that?"

"Don't act so innocent. I've seen you come and go out of his office for a year, usually at night. What else goes down at night in a professor's office, Catalina?"

Her lower lip trembles. She pins him with her eyes. "You really wanna know that fuckin' bad?" Her eyes fills with tears. "See that grave over there." She points to where she was standing earlier. "That right there is the reason I see the professor every night. You think I have the luxury like most of the students here? The professor gave me a job, if you must know. One I've kept quiet about this entire time until you assholes showed up. So, no Cole, I'm not sleeping with my professor."

She walks over to her gear, grabs her shovel, and goes back to digging.

"Why is she digging?" Nyx looks so confused. I shrug because what the fuck do I know. We stand around watching while she digs this grave.

"Did you want help or anything? I feel horrible just standing by while you work so hard?"

She looks so tiny in the hole she's digging; she pops her head up looking at me. "I'm good. I do this more than you think. I'm almost there, anyway. You don't have to dig the entire six feet, only to the top of the coffin."

"I'll take your word for it, considering this is the first time I'm seeing anyone dig up a body."

Cole stands clenching his jaw muscle. While Nyx looks like he's going to throw up considering, he can kill a person yet this is drawing the line. I find this fascinating, like how cool is it to have this as a job. Don't get me wrong I enjoy beating the shit out of people, but hers she's always on high alert to never get caught. The adrenaline that must be pumping through her body. I feel myself harden under those thoughts.

Her small grunt brings me out my thoughts. "Can someone hand me the rope and hooks? Maybe I'll use your help after all. I'm getting tired."

I move forward searching the tarp for what she needs. When I look down at her, she's covered in dirt. She straps the hooks up under the armpits and lifts her hand up to me. Grinning at her I hike her upwards. She's so small and light it doesn't take much effort.

"There you go, half pint. Want me to pull it up for you?"

She bites her lower lip. "Fine, only cause it's late, and you guys crashed my night yet again."

I've never hauled a dead body out of a coffin. Let me tell you it was interesting.

"Are you going to tell us why you do this?" Cole demands.

"Seriously. I can't catch a break with you, can I? Why else would someone dig up a body?" She glares at him.

"I can't tell you; you are already weird. This could be a cult thing."

"I'm weird. You guys live in a house with skulls, and shit hanging on your walls. So, get over yourself. Oh, and what's your gang called. *Soul Stealers.*" She rolls her eyes. "How stupid. Did a kindergartener name it?"

He's on her so fast she didn't have time to move. He grabs her throat lowering his face to hers. "You watch your mouth. That gang you speak of could do anything they want to you."

"I'm not afraid. I've been through far worse than you can imagine, so take your boys and leave me alone." She narrows her eyes.

He releases her. Never letting her move out of the way.

"You're a prick you know that." Shoving past him, she works quickly bundling the body in the bag and packing up her tools. She swings her satchel over her head. Bending down, she grabs the body bag then starts dragging it towards her van.

I swing back to Cole. "What the hell was that? We're trying to get on her good side, and you go off and fucking grab her by the throat. Are you kidding me right now?"

"Watch your fucking mouth. Do you forget who's the boss around here?"

I go in to show him who really is the fucking boss.

"Hey, hey. That's enough you two." Nyx pushes his body between the both of us. "Stop right now. This isn't like us, we've never let a woman get to us before."

Cole steps back throwing his hands up. "You're right, we aren't, she's done. Don't touch, talk or associate with her anymore. She's tearing us apart and hells if I'm letting a woman do that to us."

"That's not what I meant at all. She didn't do anything wrong. That's on us," I told him.

He shakes his head. "It's done. She wanted us to stop anyway, so." He walks away, I watch as he walks right past Cat who's still dragging her body bag. She doesn't even look at him, I'm pretty sure she heard our fight. It wasn't like we were quiet.

"Let's go. He can cool off at home. Besides, we have a job to that needs to be finished. As shitty as that is to say." Nyx strolls away, stopping to talk to Cat but she waves him off.

How did this night turn into a shit storm? I stop at Cat's side.

"Did you want any help? I'm sorry for how this night ended. That wasn't how it was supposed to go."

She waves me off, too. "Don't worry about me. I'm a big girl. Go they need you."

I know I should stay, but she's right; they do need me, but I wanted her to need me too. We need a way to all get over our shit. I want her, Nyx wants her, but fucking Cole. He'll take the most to convince otherwise. He doesn't have a problem getting his dick sucked, but God forbid if he gets his feelings involved.

With Coles' wishes, it's been a week since we've all talked to Catalina. Nyx still sees her in class, but they both ignore each other. I can tell it's killing him. It would kill me, too. Instead, we pushed ourselves into doing what we do best. As always, Henry is still having us drive around. I have no clue why it's bullshit. We already destroyed one drug house; I highly doubt we have anymore that are going to pop up anytime soon. He's just being paranoid now, like how much control does one really need over this town. We were about to call it quits when Cole's phone goes off. He's reaching for his personal phone when he goes for his back pocket, it's his burner so we know it's new job.

He lowers his head pressing his palm into his eye. Great, this is going to be a shit job. I just know it. He hangs up, lets out a few mumbles.

"You're not going to like the new job."

"Why? Another drug house?" I deadpanned.

He blows out a heavy breath, his face rumpled with doubt. "Henry wants to know why the graves are being dug up."

"Fuck," Nyx whispered.

"Oh, shit," I mumbled.

"Yeah. Catalina found herself on the wrong side of the gang. I don't know what to do."

If Henry wants someone, it's only a matter of time. Especially if he calls us. He's not going to let this go, he'll want someone brought in because what he wants, he wants delivered promptly. There's only one thing I can think of doing.

"We're gonna have to protect her now, you do realize that. I'm not handing her over for something that she does for work. Fuck Henry."

They both nod, the only question is how. We can't come out and tell her can we? Her life is going to be at risk now, Henry will know something is up.

"I'll come up with a plan, let's head home for the night. We'll try to talk with her at school," Cole said.

"Yeah, if she will. She doesn't even look at me in class anymore. I think we really hurt her."

Nyx looks troubled. Shaking his head, he starts his bike. If anyone can get through to Cat, it'll be him.

He's the friendly one out the bunch. I can only hope he can get her to listen.

9

CATALINA

The guys have left me alone for a week, a week of pure bliss.

Okay, that's a lie. I missed when Nyx would look at me, or how Cole would dominate me and how Dorian would protect me, and they each have their own nicknames for me. Like how pathetic is that. Who falls for their bullies? It has to happen more than often, right? Or is it trauma from my childhood that I'm holding onto? Either way, I think I'm falling for each one of them and them being quiet has really shown me that I've looked forward to them every day since school started. Is it normal to want three lovers?

"Jesus Cat, you sound like a fucking pussy." Why am I always talking to myself? "Probably because you have no friends."

I really don't. I have a hard time trusting people. After what her sons put me through, I can't tell what people's motives are. I continue on with my painting, brush to canvas is the best therapy around. I close my eyes as I paint. I don't need to see when you paint in abstract; I trust my hand to lead. My piece I'm working on is called *Wrath*. I wish I could show it towards her sons. I'll never have the chance because hells if I'm ever going back there. I'll paint it out instead. I dip my brush into the red, creating nice long strokes on the canvas.

I've been working on my art for most of the day, this piece is due in a week, and I need to buckle down to finish it in time. It's my own fault for slacking, my mind has been elsewhere. I can't keep thinking about them, they left me not the other way around and it's not like we were all in a relationship together. They got me off a couple of times and vice versa. It should be easy to forget and walk away, so why can't I?

I need another job, that's what I need. The professor has had nothing in days. I can't stay inside the walls of my apartment any longer can't somebody die so I can get some work. I get how bad that sounds, but come on *already*. Karma is probably going to bite me in the ass for that remark. My phone dings with a text. Only one person ever sends me a text. Dr. Deadbodies. Looks like I have a job tonight after all, see. That's what happens when you think hard enough, things happen.

The job is out in Eaglewood, thank the lucky stars. Be a little more relaxed than in town that's for sure.

I wouldn't have to look over my back continuously. Get in, get out. Never know I could be home early enough to enjoy a nice warm bath, the evenings are getting a little chillier. Packing up my art I head out. The parking lot is almost empty, considering it's damn near four o'clock. The sun is setting reflecting a nice orange hue on the windshields of the few vehicles in the lot. I shield my eyes looking around to make sure I'm alone. I don't need anyone following me to the medical parking lot. No point going home just to turn around to come back again, I'll have to drop a few things off at my car first. I take a step onto the pavement, only to hear a rev of a bike entering the parking lot.

I continue making my way to my car without paying whoever is rolling in any attention. Digging in my bag for my keys, the revving grows louder. I slam my keys into the lock getting it unlocked in no time. Sometimes I wish this car had a remote.

"Wednesday, we need to talk." There was an edge to Cole's voice. I should've known it was him.

I smack my head against my car window a few times before rotating in his direction. Cole has his arms resting over his handlebars, his jet-black hair is tousled from the wind. He never takes his icy-blue eyes off me. His biceps flex catching my eyes, that dirty bastard knows exactly what he's doing to me.

"The fuck do you want Cole," I snapped, getting frustrated with every second he's wasting.

"Where ya headed?"

"Why the sudden interest in my life? You leave me alone for what a week? Just needed to torment me is that it?" I turn around opening my door.

"That's not it Catalina. Look, I'm sorry for being a real asshole to you—"

"Seriously." I storm closer to him. "That's how you're going to apologize, you take something out of context and that's that. You are unreal." Rage roars through me, I clench my hand into a fist. Rearing my arm back, I punch him in that handsome face of his. The crunching sound tells me I fucked up. The pain that shoots up my arm. Tells me I broke something for sure. Too bad it wasn't on him. Sweet baby Jesus.

I stagger backwards, holding my hand to my chest. Tears roll down my cheeks from the pain that's shooting down my arm.

"Jesus Wednesday, what were you thinking." Cole's hand wraps around mine. I hiss when he tries to move it.

"Clearly I wasn't thinking ass. I wanted to hurt you."

"You forget how tiny you are. Come on, we gotta get you to the hospital."

I shake my head. "I can't, I have a job I have to do tonight." Wincing when I try to flex my fingers. Maybe I didn't break anything, I could've just sprained them. Right?

"Don't be stupid. Get in the car, I'll drive. Now."

This wasn't how I seen my evening going, if it wasn't for him I could've been digging a body right now. He ruins everything. Climbing into the car I have to laugh. Watching a six-foot man trying to sit into my seat is the best thing ever.

"How the hell can you drive this thing?" He grunts trying to reposition the seat.

"Well, it helps when you're short, how do you ride that bike of yours?"

"Easy, fast." He smirks as he pulls out of the parking spot.

I shake my head aggressively. "Pass. I like the comfort of four tires on the ground."

"Ahh, once you feel that vibration between those legs of yours, you'll be hooked, Wednesday."

Butterflies perform a dance in my lower stomach. I squeeze my thighs together when I picture what the thought of him and I on his bike would look like.

The drive to the hospital is quiet, I don't know what I'm going to do. My scholarship is running on my grades. If I can't complete my art project, I'll fail. Say goodbye to my funds. Then I can't work. Jesus, what the fuck was I thinking. I have to hold back tears and pray that it's only fractured or bruised. No damage please. I send a mental prayer to whoever listens to non-believers.

"Come on, you got lucky and no more going around punching people in the face for now on."

I toss him a side eye. "You are the lucky one, if I ended up with a broken finger I would be fucked right about now. Consider yourself lucky, asshole. Now go grab your bike. I can handle getting home."

My hand is in a brace. I'm looking at a sprained middle finger, but I'll sacrifice everything just to punch him again.

"Really? That's how you want to end the night. I actually came here to tell you something not for you to attack me."

"I wouldn't have had to attack you if you weren't such a dickhole."

He lets out a groan. "You are being unreasonable. I came here to tell you to watch yourself."

"Oh, cause that doesn't sound threatening in any way." I shift in my seat, placing my back against the car door.

"I'm only trying to help Wednesday. Hand me your phone." He reaches across holding his hand out. Not letting me have a choice in the matter.

I've never taken notice to how much larger his hand is compared to mine. I feel like a child sitting next to him, no wonder why Dorian calls me half pint. I reach into my bag and fumble around, it's a lot harder with one hand. I slam my phone into his palm with a grin. I watch him add his number into my phone. He passes it back to me with a smirk.

"Call if anything happens." He opens his door and steps out.

I didn't even notice we were back at school, I was too busy checking him out or fantasizing about punching him still. Now for him to leave so I can get to work, this is going to take some maneuvering. I can't afford to let Dr. Deadbodies know I can't do this job. The rev of his engine brings me out of my head, I climb out of the car walking to the driver's side.

"Behave tonight Wednesday."

"Same to you, and whatever you get up to with your gang of merry men." I salute him before getting into Johnny. I wait until he leaves before getting out and walking to my van.

I don't know why he felt the need to warn me. I haven't gotten into trouble before and I don't plan on finding it now. *Great,* now I'm going to be paranoid all fuckin' night. Thanks a lot, Cole. If anything, they don't know I take jobs in Eaglewood, it's my only hiding spot. For now.

It's later than I wanted to start, by the time we left the hospital it was nine. I wanted to be home by now, there goes my relaxing bath this evening. Parking my van as close to the grave I try to think how I'm going to do this. How much damage can I do if I take my brace off? Fuck it, gonna have to try it without it. I can't make a fist without it bringing me to tears. Please let this body be a lightweight.

It's been two hours and I'm still digging; I'm not even halfway done. I don't think I have the energy to finish it. Sitting down I stare down at the grave. How is it you live your entire life only to end up here in a hole in the ground covered in dirt. *What a joke.*

I force myself to dig, the amount of pain I'm in is making my head throb. With every sink of the shovel, my finger swells. Maybe I should've left the brace on.

"Well, no one said you were smart." I whimpered when I try to continue. Finally, my shovel hits the coffin.

"Sweet fuckin' Jesus." I'm almost finished. My chest is heaving, my left hand is working overtime pulling the rope. I think I'll have to tell Dr. Dead-bodies that I'll need the week off, I have no choice. With determination, I get this job done.

Wheeling the gurney into the cooler seals the rest of my night. I'm done, I can't do it anymore. My hand is throbbing in pain. I'm scared to look under the brace, guaranteed I fucked it up worse. The walk back to my car is quiet, almost too quiet. Usually, some form of bird is out flying no matter what time of day. I pick up my pace, I have better things to do then let my brain wander. My car is only a few feet away when a black figure steps out from behind it. I stumble to a stop. A flicker of a light can be seen under the hood, then all I see is a LED light up mask. Just like what the guys wore. Except this one isn't their colour, it's yellow.

I move my hand under the flap of my bag so I can get my phone.

"I wouldn't move if I were you," he spat out in a low, croaky voice.

I try to swallow the lump that's quickly forming. "Who are you?"

He steps away from my car; I see something reflect in his hand. My heart hammers in my chest, my hand twitches in my bag, feeling the outline of my phone. If I can only grab it, I only have a few contacts. Someone will come if they figure out where I am.

"What are you doing out so late pretty girl? Don't you know by now that strangers come out at night?"

Those words are so familiar it's scary. My boys said something almost the same Halloween night while wearing the same masks. Was someone watching us? My fight-or-flight kicks in, I still have the keys to the door for the school. It'll be my best shot.

I take off, running full tilt my feet pounding on the pavement. My breath comes out in pants as I try to get away, I hear his feet pounding behind me. I don't know who he is or what he wants, but he isn't going to get it. Running and fishing into a bag takes a lot of concentration, and coordination.

"Get back here you bitch," He yelled. His voice closer than I would like.

Who is this guy? I don't remember pissing anyone off, nor talking to anyone at school lately. I always stick to myself. So why am I a target? The door is right there, only two feet from me when I'm thrown to the ground with him on top of me. My sore hand smashing to the pavement. I yell out in pain. Even with the brace on, I can feel everything. With everything I have, I throw my elbow back connecting with his face, which caused him to fall backwards. I roll onto my knees climbing to my feet I take off in a clumsy run.

"HELP!" I scream even though I know there's no one around, but your assaulter never likes to be called out. I dig around in my bag again when I feel my lanyard. I yank it free from my purse I slam the key fob onto the keyless entry system.

"Hurry, turn green." Why does the seconds seem to take forever when you're running for your life? When the red light finally turns green, I swing open the door, pulling it closed faster. The masked man slams into it, pulling on the handle. Luckily for me, it locks automatically.

He slams his hand on the window that's holding the knife. My body trembles as he stares at me, the glow from his mask lighting up his eyes. I slowly back up.

"I'll be seeing you, Catalina; you best be watching your back." The yellow neon lights flick off, submitting him to the darkness of the night.

My chin wobbles, I close my eyes trying to calm myself down. When the first tear falls, I sink down the wall. Bringing my knees to my chest I let them fall freely. Sometimes it's okay not to be strong. How did my life become such a rollercoaster? With a shaky hand, I grip my phone.

It rings and rings. I sniff back more tears as I hang up. Isn't that great. Now I'll have to call Dr. Deadbodies and try to explain this entire situation. I don't even know this situation. Maybe it'll be safe to go outside.

"Either you're stupid or have a death wish." I whisper to myself. Both are up in the air.

Turning on the flashlight on my phone, gripping my keys I peer out the window not that I can see much, but I can see enough to know he's not hanging around. With a deep breath, I push the door open.

"And you wonder why the cat died, Catalina." Guess I'm not that smart.

Scanning the parking lot, I don't see a soul. I'm still on edge. What if he did another jack-in-the box appearance. I quicken my pace without trying to freak myself out.

"No, the boogeyman doesn't exist, Cat." I swivel my head around checking, anyway.

When I reach my car, I could cry all over again. I try calling Cole again.

"Pick up, pick up assho—"

"Hello," his raspy voice cut me off.

Emotion welled in my throat when I tried to talk.

"Hello, who's there?" Irritation surged him.

"C-Cole," I gasped wetly.

"Catalina?"

"I didn't know who else to call."

"Hey, that's okay. What's wrong? What happened?"

I take an unsteady breath. "I'm still at the school. Can you come get me."

I hear him getting out of bed. "Yeah, give me about twenty minutes. Hang tight. Are you sure you're, okay?"

I shake my head, then realize he can't see. "No," I whispered.

"Hold on." Then he hangs up.

I sit by my car touching my one slashed tire. "We had a good run didn't we, hey?"

I close my eyes and wait. I want this nightmare to end.

10

C⚬LE

I stumble out of bed, pulling pants on then go knocking on the guys' door, waking their asses up.

Dorian flings his door open red faced. "What the hell, man."

Nyx stumbles out of his room, pulling his sweats on.

"No time. Catalina's in trouble. Let's go." Skipping the stairs two at a time, I run into the kitchen to grab my car keys. No time for the bikes.

"What exactly happened?" Nyx asked rounding the corner to the kitchen.

I can only shrug. "I have no idea. She didn't go into detail, she sounded scared, and she was crying. Now I'm glad I gave her my number."

"Less talking, more action. She could still be in danger." Dorian grabs the keys from my hands heading for the front door.

"What the hell is happening in this town, Cole?"

That's what I would like to know, it used to be so laid back, Henry has some questions to be asking that fuckin' mayor of ours. We've never had any attacks at night before, hence why we had fuckin' purge night on Halloween.

What usually took twenty minutes Dorian got us there in ten. I knew where she was parked, so I gave him directions. The parking lot was dimly lit, unfortunately for Catalina she never parked under a light. Her car sat alone in the deserted lot. All I could make out was the shape of her black Volkswagen Beetle.

"Something's wrong with her car." Nyx points out. "Look at her rear tire. It's flat."

"Maybe that's why she called. Could be, cause she doesn't know how to change a flat tire."

"I don't think so. No one cries that much over a tire. Besides, you would call a tow truck, wouldn't you?" I shift in my seat trying to get a closer look at her car. I can't see her; I'm hoping she's smart enough to be inside of it.

Dorian parks behind it. As we all climb out, we take in our surrounding.

"Shit." I can hear Nyx whisper.

Shit is right, the driver's side reveals both tires are slashed, along with the words WEDNESDAY scratched into the door panel.

"What the hell, I've only ever heard you call her that and only when we were together," Dorian utters, making sure no one could hear him.

"Catalina?" Nyx called out quietly.

A small whimper comes from the other side of the car. Rounding the front of the car I find her sitting against the passenger side door, knees curled to her chest cradling her braced hand. Kneeling in front of her I place my hand on her knee. She jerks her head up, her eyes are bloodshot and puffy. Tears fall from her left eye. Her hair messy bun sitting lopsided on her head.

"Wednesday, baby what happened?" I stroke her cheek, wiping her tears away. Her lower lip trembles. She looks between all of us then bursts into heavy cry.

"I-I... tried to c-call you earlier." Her voice shook. Regret washes over me. If only I heard my phone ring the first time. We could've gotten here sooner.

I stand only to scoop her into my arms. "Come, let's get you home." She rests her head on my chest. She looks so small in my arms.

"Do you need anything from your car?" Dorian questions her.

"No, just grab my bag." Her small voice answered him. Pointing to the ground, where her bag lays.

I lock eyes with Dorian. He'll know to check the car for anything suspicious. Nyx opens the passenger door for me helping me slide in. Brushing her hair away from her face, I lean down placing a kiss on her forehead. Her body is cold. I lightly rub my hand up and down her arm.

"Are you hurt anywhere?"

She winces when she moves her hand. "I smashed my hand into the ground when I was pushed, I haven't looked yet."

"We'll do it at the house, relax you're safe now with us."

She closes her eyes. Her small hand runs up my chest working around my neck, running her fingers through my hair.

I didn't think that small movement would calm me so much, nor did I know it's what I needed at this moment. I'm the one that should be helping her feel calm, not the other way around. I pull her closer giving her more warmth.

The front two doors slam shut making her hand still. "Ready?" Dorian spoke faintly while starting the car. We all remain quiet on the drive home. Guilt eats me alive; I should've done more. I could've stayed with her tonight. Did I honestly have to leave her? I press my lips into her hair inhaling her scent.

"Wanna tell us what happened?" I asked her. When we arrived home, we've gathered in the living room. I'm kneeling in front of her waiting for her answer. I grab her hand not knowing what to expect under her brace. Undoing the Velcro, she takes a deep inhale. "If it hurts too much, we can go back to the hospital."

"No, it's okay. It's just the relief of all the pressure I think."

I continue undoing the brace, I gently slide it off. "I don't see any more damage, but it's swollen."

"That would be my fault. I didn't wear it when I was digging."

"Here you go, baby." Nyx places a bag of ice on her hand. She tilts her head up smiling at him. He cups her face placing a gentle kiss to her rosy lips. The sight of them kissing causes my dick to twitch. When he pulls away, he smiles. "When you're ready can you tell us?"

"Way to kill the moment, Nyx." She laughed as he shrugged, she closes her eyes taking a deep breath. "After I was finished tonight someone was standing by my car, wearing the same masks you guys were wearing." Opening her eyes tears cling to her eyelashes. "He said some things that sounded the same to what you said on that night. It's like he's watching us."

"What the fuck?" Dorian whispered, uneasiness creeping into his voice.

Now I understand why her nickname was scratched into her car. "Did he try to hurt you?" Nyx asked, mindfully.

She shakes her head. "I was able to run inside the school, I have a key. Thank God."

I rub small circles on her knees. As she lets out a small yawn. I can only imagine how tired she is. She's been through a lot tonight. All I know is I'm claiming her tonight before those two can. I have a great deal to make up for.

"Come on, I'll take you to bed." I reach for her hand standing I help her off the couch.

She searches between the three of us. "Go with Cole, baby. He needs you tonight." Nyx insists, placing a kiss to her forehead before heading upstairs.

Dorian comes over placing another kiss to her forehead. "Good night darling, see you in the morning."

"Are you okay sharing a bed with me?"

"Of course. Thank you for coming to get me. I didn't know who else to call."

I lead her up the stairs. "We'll make sure you always have someone to call from now on, don't ever feel guilty for calling us, I only wish I've gotten there sooner." Wrapping my arm around her waist I pull her into my side. I lead her up one more flight of stairs to my floor. It's more so the attic of the house, but it's still nice having it all to myself.

When she enters my room, it's with pure amazement on her face. "Oh, wow. This is beautiful."

My room isn't anything special. There's a queen-sized bed in the middle of the room, across from the bed is my dresser with a tv mounted over top. When she turns her head to the right she gasps.

"Is that a bathtub in your room?"

I chuckle. "Ah yes, that would be my tub." She's referring to my claw-foot tub that sits for everyone to see, what I love most about it is when I can see who's in it. "Don't worry you can try it later. Right now, I have other plans." I walk her towards my bed until her legs hit the edge, causing her to sit.

"Arms up. I'll help you get undressed." When she raises her arms, she gives me a small smile. I'm drawn into her violet eyes. I run my hands down her ribs, reaching for the hem of her shirt. I pull it up slowly running my hands along her smooth skin. She closes her eyes when I touch her breasts. Pulling her shirt over her head we lock eyes again.

"Why did it take me so long to find you?"

She whispered, "Maybe cause you were looking in all the wrong places."

"I'm not letting you go. You're mine now Wednesday."

"I'm all of yours." She wraps her arms around my waist, resting her forehead on my stomach. I thread my fingers in her hair, closing my eyes, enjoying this moment. I didn't think it would be possible to have her in my arms. I thought I fucked it all up when I misjudged her.

"Will you forgive me?" I asked her.

She looks up at me with narrowed brows. "What do you mean?"

"For the way I treated you, it wasn't fair. I judged you before I knew you, then we got into a fight. I should've stayed or done something. That prick touched what's mine. He's dead when I find him."

"Cole, what happened tonight isn't your fault. Whoever followed me must've been doing it for a while, we need to figure out who it is."

I need to talk to Henry first thing, this has him written all over. Then again, he only just mentioned about someone digging up bodies, so can it be him?

"Enough of this conversation. I have plans remember." I push her on her back dipping my fingers into her waistband. "Are you okay with this?"

"Yes," she whispered.

I pull her leggings off, leaving her in another pair of Halloween thong. I cock my eyebrow up.

She laughed. "What can I say? I love Halloween."

"I can see this. What will it take to see something sexy on this body of yours?"

"Don't know, don't own sexy underwear."

I tsk at her. "We'll have to change that, I need to see this body in something with leather." I kiss her inner thigh, moving upwards, I move past her needy pussy and work upwards her stomach. She lets out a muffled moan. I wrap my hands around the straps of her bra sliding them down her arms, I slide her bra off her breasts.

I reach around her back unclasping her bra. Her nipples tighten when the cool air hit them. Her body looks so dainty under my massive size, I have to remind myself that she can't handle my entire body weight at once. My hand swallows her breast easily, rubbing her nipple between my finger and thumb she pushes her hips into my stomach, moaning as she does.

"That feels good."

I find her other nipple bringing it into my mouth, sucking it before I bite it.

"Holy fuck," she screamed.

"You like that? I know you don't like being tied, but can we try something different?"

Her breath hitches. "I don't know Cole, I need to feel like I can get away."

"Trust me." I take her hands being careful of her sore one, guiding them to the headboard. "Hold on, don't let go or the fun stops."

She nods. Grabbing onto the spindles of the head-board with her good hand, laying her bad hand on the mattress.

"That's my good girl."

I repeat the process to her other breast. I dip my finger into her panties.

"Mmm, you're so wet. What are you thinking of?" I swipe my finger along her clit.

"You," she moaned.

"Doing what?" I swipe once more.

"Fucking me. I want to know what it feels like to have you inside of me."

God, I want to know too. I hook my fingers into her panties peeling them off. I stand pulling my shirt off over my head, I push my sweats down standing naked with a throbbing hard-on. She licks her lips; pupils fully blown out with lust and need. I grab the bag of ice that she used for her hand. Finding a piece, I kneel on the bed spreading her legs.

"Don't let go. Red is your safe word." I wait for her nod, then ever so slowly drag the ice cube up her shin, she lets out a gasp when the ice touches her skin. Her skin breaks out in goosebumps. I only end up with wicked thoughts, it's hard to control the inner demons. They only want to come out and play. They wanted to come out on Halloween, but she wasn't ready for them. I can smell her arousal letting me know she's ready. After being with Dorian and Nyx, I'm sure she can handle me.

I continue to run the ice cube on her body, running it around her belly button, her heals dig into the bed for leverage when I leave the ice cube sitting collecting water in her belly button. I fish another ice cube from the bag, suck her right nipple in my mouth she squirms under my body. I draw back watching her nipple tighten even more from the cool air. I blow warm air over it.

"Cole, please."

Her hand squeezes the frame harder, her hips grinding onto my groin. "God, you feel good." I drag the ice cube around her nipple, watching it pucker even more. Kissing down her stomach I remove the ice cube from her belly button. Dipping my tongue into the pool of water that has collected, I dip my finger inside her wet entrance, curling my fingers touching her g-spot. I drink the water from her button before moving lower.

11

CATALINA

Oh, my fucking God.

My body is on fire. With every touch from Cole, I feel like I'm going to combust. The dip of his tongue into my belly button shouldn't be this hot. The swipe of his tongue on my clit has me fighting my orgasm.

"Come for me little one." His demands sends me over the edge. I pulsate around his finger as I come.

He pushes another finger in while sucking my clit. My entire body shaking, he's the only one I haven't had sex with, and the anticipation is killing me. I understand why he hasn't I wouldn't want him anywhere near me, but now that we resolved our differences nothing can stand in our way.

A shiver runs up my leg followed by wetness; he slowly slides the ice cube up my inner thigh.

"You use those safe words if this gets too much."

"Okay."

"Are you on birth control?" His lips nip at my nape.

"Yes."

He rests his head taking a deep breath. "Thank fuck, I need to feel you so bad." He sits up, spreading my legs, exposing my pussy for him. He groans, I jump when he touches me with a ice cube on my clit.

"How does that feel?"

"G-Good." My hand grips the spindle till my knuckles turn white.

Then he shoves the ice cube inside of me. "Hold it, don't let it fall out."

I hiss from the shock, squeezing my inner walls around something cold sends my body into overdrive. I've never done something like this before. Sex has always been vanilla for me. Squeezing as the ice melts water drips out. Cole's sculpted body is on show for me, his deep v lines showing me exactly what I'm about to receive. Cole strokes himself, his piercings glimmering in the faint light. I've never felt a pierced cock before. He slowly leans forward lining up.

"What about the ice?"

He smirks. "Don't you worry about that." He runs his piercing along my clit, before finding my wet entrance, he slowly nudges his way in, stretching me. "Oh, fuck, you're so tight holding that ice. I'm going to fuck this ice right out of you."

He pushes the rest of the way in. My scream is silent as I feel everything. The sensation is unlike anything I've felt before. The warmth of his cock mixed with the coldness of the ice.

"That's right." *Thrust.* "Take." *Thrust.* "Everything." He told me between thrusts. I reach down grabbing his ass to get him deeper when he stops. I let out a whine.

"What did I tell you about letting go?" He pulls out, flipping me over onto my knees. "You need to listen little one. Hands out front."

Smack. Then another ice cube is placed inside. "Cole, holy shit."

"You can take it; I know you can." Then he slams back into me with much more force. I come immediately. Clamping around him with a force that he groans and digs his fingers into my hips, pulling me closer. My knees are trembling to keep me up. His thrusts become ruthless, his hands coming to my shoulders as he brings his feet onto the bed. He only becomes more savage this way. My lower stomach tightens again. I hide my head into the bed and scream closing my eyes tight. I see stars, I chase my release until I'm struggling to stay on my knees. Cole speeds ups before pulling out and coming all over my back.

"You look good covered in my cum." He draws swirls in his cum, then I collapse on the bed.

My eyelids are like bricks. I can't keep them open anymore. I'm on a high. I didn't even pay attention when Cole cleaned off my back or when he pulled me into his chest. The kisses he leaves on my shoulder feels like a distance.

"Feeling okay Wednesday?"

"Yeah, tired and sore."

He rubs my neck and into my hair. "Sore in a good way?"

"Yes, and no. My hand is starting to throb again. I need to get my brace on." He rolls away leaving the room. I get up making my way to the bathroom. When I get back into the bedroom, Cole is sitting on the bed. He glances up and down, that's when I realize I'm still naked.

He takes my hand slipping my brace on, kissing my exposed knuckles. "Let's get you to bed. We have a lot to figure out in the morning."

I never thought sleeping in the same bed with someone would make me feel so safe before. I never wanted to rely on anyone to make me feel this way especially after her sons terrorized me. I felt like I couldn't trust anybody ever again. They completely ruined me.

"Shh, I got you. Everything will be okay." He wipes a tear that's streaming down my cheek. That's when I realized I've been crying, how dare those assholes get my tears. I cuddle closer, closing my eyes.

We're all sitting around the kitchen table while Dorian cooks breakfast. Bacon crisping on the stove, while he flips pancakes, it seems a little too homey for me. This wasn't how this was supposed to be. How did we end up here, anyway? I'm looking at each one of them. They are chatting, drinking coffee like it's a regular morning. I've never been around such normalcy I'm not sure how I'm supposed to act. Is this a normal thing for people to do every morning? I've only ever seen this in movies. These three have a strong bond I've never seen before. To be honest, it's a beautiful sight to see.

"How long have you known each other?" My eyes darting around the room looking at each one.

"Dorian and I knew each other since elementary school. Then we met Cole in junior high," Nyx said looking at them with a heartfelt smile.

"That's a real long ass time."

"Doesn't seem that long when you think about it, we've been through a lot of shit together. I wouldn't have it any other way." Dorian smiles over his shoulder.

Guess that's what I'm really missing in life, a friendship. I've always been classified as the *weird* one in school that no one wanted to become friends with. I've let it grow the older I've gotten. If no one wanted to be friends with me, that was fine.

Dorian places the food on the table before sitting next to me. His hand resting on my thigh, inching under the t-shirt that I'm wearing, he places a pancake on my plate followed by some bacon.

"Eat please," he whispered in my ear, sending shivers down my spine. I have a hard time concentrating on anything with him sitting this close to me.

"All right, we need to figure out what the fuck went down last night. Do you have any enemies?"

I can feel Cole's eyes on me, but I continue to stare at my pancakes. Do I have enemies? I don't think so. Why would I? I always stick to myself, and I bug no one. I shake my head. "No, I never talk to anyone around campus. I go to class, then back to my apartment. I never disrupt anyone."

"What about your art? Has anyone been pissed off because you've excelled more than them?" This time, Nyx asked the question. Concern written all over his face.

"Again, not that I can think of. I wouldn't classify myself as the best painter." I hitch my shoulders. My forehead creasing as I think of someone. "I honestly don't know who this could be. What about one of you? It could be someone you know."

All three lean back at the same time, when they realize that it could be them.

"Well, shit I didn't think of that. We've pissed off so many people it's not even funny." Nyx rubs the back of his neck, bringing his hand around rubbing his chin. "What if she's right?"

"If she's right, then we have our work cut out for us." Dorians shoulder slump forwards.

Cole only sits there staring straight ahead not saying or doing anything.

Only stewing.

"Cole," I say his name in a low whisper. He slowly cocks his head in my direction. His blue eyes hardening when they land on me.

"I think it's time for you to head home. One of us will give you a ride" His voice is low but stern.

I flinch. This can't be from the same person that just took me to bed last night, the one that apologized because he was in the wrong. Can it?

"What the hell, Cole?" Dorian demanded. "She didn't do anything wrong. Where is this coming from?"

Cole narrows his gaze on Dorian. "I want her out."

You know what? I know when I'm wanted and clearly this isn't it. I thought this was going to be different. I rise from the table never taking my eyes off Cole.

"You know what Cole, I regret everything. All of it. You, them... all of it. I thought this was going to be different. You are just like every other guy out there. Once you get it, you turn into a complete asshole." It makes him flinch, but he says nothing.

Dorian reaches for me, but I pull out of his grip. Nyx stands looking like a lost puppy. Fuck them. I'll find my own way home. I march upstairs to Cole's room, throwing on my clothes and grabbing my bag. Dorian and Nyx are waiting by the front door when I come down.

"Don't listen to him, he's just upset that's all." Nyx pleads with me.

I give him a clipped nod. "Sure, he is, what happens next time? He says something again because something pisses him off. I'm not dealing with that. I don't need someone in my life that can't figure out what he wants or to wait till he grows the fuck up. Sorry, but I can't do this."

Dorian hangs his head. I feel bad because in return I have to punish these two. It's not fair, but I can't keep two knowing that they still talk to him. I grab the doorknob.

"I'll drive you," Dorian told me.

"That's fine. I called a ride." They don't need to know I didn't, I need to walk all this built up energy off. Pulling the door open I step outside saying goodbye to what I thought was going to be the best thing of my life.

12

CATALINA

It's been a week since I've talked to any of the guys. Nothing but radio silence from all of them. Which I understand that's how I wanted it.

They haven't been at school since I walked out of their house, not sure if that's Coles doing or mine. I've been trying to ignore them, too. Guess I'm still trying to figure out what the hell happened between Cole and me. We were fine and all of a sudden. Boom. He went off on me. It's like he did a one eighty.

My finger is healed so I'm able to go back to work. It helps so I can't think as much. I had to take an extension on my art project, I can't express words for how grateful I am. My piece turned out better than I could imagine. Probably because I have all this pent-up anger inside. I'm also going to assume one of the boys had my car fixed for me, because Johnny was parked right outside of my apartment a few days after I walked out of their house. Now I have to find the finances to pay them back. I don't want to owe them any favours.

I'm sitting in my Philosophy class, trying to listen to Professor Adams, but his voice sounds so dry today. Who cares about other people when my entire world is crashing around me. I have problems going on too you know. Bigger than what he's trying to preach. I sound like a sad sack, they clearly got what they wanted and are now done with me, so why am I still so obsessed with them. It's not like I ever gave them a time of day before, so it shouldn't matter now. I need to either drown myself in paint or a grave. Right about now, I'd take the grave. I need to physically wear myself out.

I'm about to pass out when the door to the classroom open, Dr. Deadbodies rushes in. I try to avoid eye contact; we made a deal that we wouldn't pay attention to each other outside of our classroom or at night if need be. The fact that he's in my classroom right now has me nervous. I didn't think him and Professor Adams are friends. He's exchanging words with Adams rather quickly and quietly. What do they have in common in this university? Dr. Deadbodies teaches biological sciences. This doesn't make any sense to me.

When he walks past me, he locks his eyes on me. A small shiver runs down my spine. I've never felt any threat from him before. I must be paranoid from my attack last week. I haven't had any more weird run-ins, although I've kept my work to a minimum and only worked once, if we're being honest. The creep could be waiting for me still, I just haven't placed myself in danger yet. He gives me a slight nod before leaving.

I do have a job tonight, I'll have to ask what the fuck was up with this. I don't like secrets.

It's freezing tonight. I bundle up extra I even pack a pair of mittens.

Heading to the school again I figured I might as well confront Dr. Deadbodies and see what the hell was going down earlier today.

"Calm the fuck down Cat." I'm a nervous wreck and I'm going to cause one. I grip my steering wheel of my poor Beetle. I've never felt this way before. I'm scanning the entire road to make sure I'm not being followed. Once I'm in my van, no one will know it's me and I'll feel a little safer. I knew I should've joined that stupid self defense class that was always being advertised around. But *no*, I thought nothing would happen to me in a dark, scary parking lot.

"Yeah well look what fucking happened, Catalina."

When I'm parked safely in the parking lot, under a streetlight, I exit my car. I wrap my coat around my body protecting myself from the night air. My nose stings from the coldness already. I hustle my ass inside, I find Dr. Deadbodies inside his office typing away on his computer. I clear my throat to get his attention.

"Oh, sorry didn't hear you come in. Sit, sit. I have something I would like to discuss with you." He sounds extra excited to see me, which calms me down.

I have no choice but to grab the seat that he wants me to claim. I lean back in the chair crossing my right leg over my left knee, tapping my finger on my knee. I raise my chin and I wait.

Then I wait. Like how *long* does it take to tell me some shit.

I stare at him, narrow my eyes. "Well, what is it?"

"I know you like digging up bodies, but with the weather turning colder sooner than expected we won't be able to work as much." I nod because he is right. "I figured you could help in the lab. I know it's not the best, but it's something."

Still doesn't answer why he was talking to the professor, but does it matter why he was talking to him? Guess it really doesn't affect me. I think about what he asked, working inside does sound amazing right about now. "When would I start?"

"Not for a few more weeks. We need stock beforehand. I get everything sorted out. Until then, you have two bodies to recover, you can space it out. But I need them here by tomorrow night. We should've been on them a few days ago."

I flex my hand, giving him a nod. He looks at my hand. "Is it better?"

"Ya, it gets a little stiff in the morning, but nothing I can't handle. I got this. I'll see you tomorrow I guess." With that, I head out.

I gather my gear, making sure the van is fully stocked once again. It's going to be weird working inside for once, and around others. That's going to be difficult for me, the talking to others and small talk. My skin crawls with the thought. My phone goes off with a text, there's only one person texting me these days, so I know exactly who's it from. Pulling it out of my bag it's directions to the graves. Both are in town.

Perfect, I don't feel like driving more than I have to.

The night is peaceful, even the wind is quiet. Nothing is moving tonight. This is how I love my mind, empty. Yet again, the grave is at the very back of the cemetery. Like always, this place gives me the chills. And I call myself a fan of all things scary.

When I open the van door a gust of wind blows inside, if that isn't a sign then I don't know what is.

"You need to get out of your head." True, serves me right for watching a horror movie last night, I'll stick with true crimes as my bedtime lullabies, apparently. The leaves crunch under my combat boots when I walk to the back of the van, a sound I've grown very fond of. It's going to suck losing that as well. I'll have to take up evening strolls like an eighty-year-old just to get my intake of fall. Then again, he knows more than I do and what's best. It's his business and I'm the employee.

Just once I would love to sell one of my painting's that would help substantially, I only need to find the right market for my work. People in Eastwood are dull and lack the taste of art, apparently. Do I need to finish school? I only came here to get away, and I received a scholarship. I could always drop out and move somewhere else get a job and start selling my work. It's not like I have anyone here holding me back.

Then the guys all pop into my mind, why I can't get them out is beyond me. It's not like we spent so much time together. We only slept together that's it. I don't owe them dick shit. But maybe it could have led to something, I could finally have my happiness with them. Don't I owe myself that at least? Not that it matters anymore they made it perfectly clear what Cole says goes.

My heart sinks more, sorta like what this shovel is doing everytime I dig in the soft earth. Am I being too soft on myself? I've been through... well we know what that is don't we?

Things are going at a slow pace. I'm not in a huge hurry tonight, like I was told, if I get everything done by tomorrow. I'm in the clear. I don't bother straining myself, I dig slower than usual, which will take me a couple of hours longer, but it's not like I have anywhere else to be. God, I sound like a sad sap. Why can't I be a better person? I just want to be happy.

"Broken record, that's what you sound like," I sang out loud. Glad no one is around to hear my horrible singing voice, my shovel hits the coffin with a thud.

Would it be wrong of me to wish for once I found treasure instead of a body? After getting out of the grave, I stand on the edge of the hole staring down at the open coffin contemplating things. That's when I hear it, a deep dark laughter.

I swivel around gripping my shovel tight. I know for a fact that my mind isn't playing games. I heard that I just can't see anything in the darkness. I crouch down low and start crawling towards my bag. If only I can get to it and grab my bear spray, I knew I should've worn it around my neck. The laughter comes again, only this time closer. With a shaky hand, I snatch the can from my bag. I study the tree line, then the tombstones behind me. The voice is in either direction, my only option is running again. I'm taking my shovel with me this time.

I race away, almost stumbling over my feet, why can't there be lights in the cemetery?

"Where are you running to pretty girl?" His voice rang out in the night.

How the hell is he finding me? I thought I lost him. I look over my shoulder in time to see a glimpse of the yellow led light of his mask dart behind a tombstone. I hide behind the closet one, my heart racing a mile a minute.

"Come out, come out wherever you are," he started singing.

I go to reach for my phone, only to realize I left it with my bag. *Fuckin' stupid idiot.* What are the odds of me getting back to my bag?

"I'm coming for you pretty girl." His voice is nearing closer to me, I need to make my move now if I'm going to do it.

I dash out, making a zig-zag pattern making it harder for him to catch me. I hear the leaves behind me crunching under his footsteps. I peer over my shoulder to see him gaining on me. It was that moment when my foot falls further than I expected. My heart bottoms out.

I fall into the grave I just dug, smacking the side of my head on the edge of the open coffin. My vision turns blurry if I move my eyes, I become dizzy if I move too quickly. I touch the side of my head wincing when I touch a bloody cut. I get up slowly when I hear that laughter again only a few feet away. I need to find that fuckin' bear spray, and of course I never got my hooks down here yet.

"Oh, come on now. You'll have to eventually get out of there. Can't stay down there forever."

I glance upwards at him; his demeanor screams he's going to do whatever he wants with me. I need to find a way to outsmart him. He's still wearing that LED mask, I can't tell what he looks like, but I can feel his eyes are on me.

"What do you want from me? I don't even know who you are?"

He laughed again. "Climb out of that hole and I'll show you who I am," he says with a sinister voice.

"Yep, I'm good down here." I move to the side that I would climb out as if I was working. He doesn't need to know I'm currently planning an escape. I may be short, but I'm a quick climber. I scan the contents of the coffin, why couldn't this one be buried with something special.

Like a thick book.

"Whatever you're planning, it's not going to work. Either way, I'll catch you."

This time, his voice comes from right above my head. I crane my neck to stare at him; I smile and flip him the middle finger.

"Fuck you."

That was the last thing I remember before my entire world went dark.

13

NYX

I'm so pissed off with Cole, I can't stand being in the same room as him.

Where does he get the right to go off on her like that? Everything was going great at breakfast until she mentioned it could be someone we know. It's not like we haven't made enemies being in Soul Stealers, but he didn't have to be an asshole to her. Here I thought we were finally making progress and then he goes and sets us back again.

"Seriously, did you have to kick her out?" Dorian asked, looking more pissed off than me.

Cole slams his hands on the kitchen table. "Yes, if it is someone, we know we're only causing her to be in more danger, I did what I thought was right." He bows his head, exhaling loud.

"I'm sure you could've done it a little better than kicking her out, especially after what you did last night, asshole." I glare at him, shaking my head.

He runs his hand through his already messy hair. "Fuck, I didn't think of that."

I scoff, walking towards the fridge. "Of course you didn't. All you thought about was yourself and trying to protect you."

His hand is around my throat pushing me into the fridge in a second. "You watch your fucking mouth; you have no idea."

"I'm pretty sure I do." I struggle to get out.

"Hey, back up man." Dorian pulls Cole away. Once his hand is off my throat, I swing.

I get one good punch to Cole's pretty face before Dorian steps in again.

"Cool it, Nyx, we understand but this isn't like you. We don't fight each other." He said the last part to Cole. "Now, I say we keep away from her for a week and see what happens. If no one attacks her, then we'll deal with it. I'm not dealing with your toddler tantrums any longer than I have to."

He storms out of the kitchen. I turn to Cole. "Figure this shit out, you have one week and that's it." We made a deal when we were in high school, if we found someone, we all liked that it was all or nothing. Well, I'm not letting him get his way. Catalina belongs with us; I can feel it, and I'm sure Dorian does, too. If only Cole can pull his head out of his ass long enough to see it.

The next day at school, I skipped my philosophy class. I couldn't stand the thought of facing Cat. If that makes me sound like a coward, so be it. I can't look her in the eyes without breaking down and beg her to come back.

Instead, I watch her from a distance.

She strolls into the classroom with her head down, her hair is braided to the side showing off her beautiful neck. She's wearing a black oversized hoodie, black leggings and her combat boots. I would be concerned about the amount of black she's wearing, but this is Catalina we're talking about, if she had shown up wearing colour then I would be worried. Not that I'm not worried. I can tell that she's taking this hard. The stupid thing is we weren't even together yet. We all felt it, though. A week is going to be torture.

I'm sitting in the warehouse while Henry tells us he has had no leads on who's digging up the bodies. We've been quiet this entire time, telling him we've been making our rounds, but haven't seen anything that looks suspicious.

They must be doing it after we leave. Is what we tell him.

He didn't like that answer. "I've given you enough time, so I hired outside help. I know you three have been busy with your schoolwork and all." Cole goes to interrupt him, but Henry holds his hand up. "Just listen. He's only here to go out after you get back in, he's not going to step on your toes. Would I do that to you after all these years?"

Honestly, yes, I don't trust him. Especially now, why wouldn't he sit us down and talk to us. This is like a slap in the face, it's telling us we can't do our job. We're only doing this to protect Catalina. We aren't stupid, he should know by now that we don't fail at any of our jobs. Why would we start now? I knew we should've found some fuckin' loser and brought him in.

"Do we get to meet this person or anything?" Dorian looked at Henry with disgust. I can tell he already hates the idea of someone stepping on our toes. Someone else in our territory. Hunting his half pint. I can read his thoughts.

Henry squints his eye at Dorian. "Not yet, boy." Dorian hates being called boy.

"Then when? This is bullshit." He slammed his fist on the table. His chest rising and falling quickly.

"You'll meet him when he finishes the job. Unless you finish before him. Either way, I want it done soon. If anyone hears what's going on in this town. It's game over."

Oh, yes, his precious town with the mayor. How can we ever forget? What happened to handing out drugs to college kids or the surrounding area. Those were the best times, now he's worried about Catalina digging up bodies for the medical class, Jesus Christ.

"I do have another job for you three. It'll take you out of town for a couple of days. I need you to check production and make sure everyone is in line."

I don't like the thought of leaving, thankfully it's only a couple of days and we should be back before the end of the week.

"Send us the details. We'll leave first thing in the morning, I doubt you have anything to worry about if they know who's boss, that is," Cole told Henry. Stroke his ego and you're in the clear.

"Very well, keep me updated and I'll see you when you get back." With that, we are dismissed.

The three of us walk out, nodding to Freddy on our way. I would love to stay and chat, but I need to clear my mind. Climbing on my black Harley, Dorian climbs onto his red one and Cole on his grey. We start them at the same time giving them a quick rev. My back tire does a spin out on the gravel before it catches traction. I shoot out of the warehouse compound like I don't give a fuck. To be honest, right about now I don't. My only concern is Catalina. If she's still digging, she might get caught and it won't be by us this time. The shitty thing is we won't be around to help her, that's what's really getting to me.

This stupid job takes us to a remote location, all because Henry wants us to check on shit. Give me a break. I call bullshit we've never had to come out here before, so why we are starting now blows my mind.

"I hate this, why couldn't he send someone else? Like, Royce. He's newer and needs to prove himself, we're the enforcers and he sends all of us out of town at the same time. This smells fishy." The way Dorian stands with his back half turned to the door; tells me he doesn't trust any of these guys.

I'm beginning to think Henry might have more information than he should. If he's been spying on our personal life, I'm having second thoughts about this gang lifestyle. This isn't what I signed up for. I don't see why it would matter if we found someone. He can't hold her over our head.

"Heads up." Cole nods towards the far door.

I notice a group of ten enter, wearing all black walking with a hand in their pockets. Guaranteed they are packing either a gun or a knife. They came here looking to cause shit, well looks like it's our lucky fuckin' day. If this doesn't make Henry happy, then I can't help him.

"Wait until they make the first move, we came to help not start shit." Cole cracks his knuckles. Waiting to get them bloody.

"Where's James?" The leader of the group calls out.

A few of the men standing around don't move, nor do they bother to call out for James. Guess they've done this before. Finally, one man steps forward.

"We're not doing this again Jayce, leave now or you'll regret your life."

"See, that's not going to work for me this time. I was promised double last time, and you failed to deliver, I paid for it and it never happened. Either hand it over." He pulls his gun out, clicks the safety off. "Or we'll simply... take it." He hitches his shoulder.

Oh, shit. Is James skimming his dealers. Dorian and Cole both stiffen at the realization that this is what happened. Son of a bitch. Henry brought us here so we would fight and make it, so he wins. He only wants the money and extra product. He knew someone was about to call him out on his shit.

"I don't like this at all," Dorian whispered.

"Same, but we have no choice. If we don't try, James' men will send word back to Henry." Cole dulled his voice down to a whisper.

"So, you want us to fight even though our side is in the wrong?" I ask, feeling disgusted even asking the question.

Cole's shoulders droop forward. "Yeah, unfortunately we don't have a choice."

Before we can do anything else, a shot is fired, and it's a mess. I whip my guns out, not knowing which side to shoot. But in the end, my gang comes first.

When we arrive home, we head straight to the warehouse, we haven't said a word to each other since we shot and killed everyone from Jayce's crew. I'm pissed and I can tell the other two are pissed. It was so uncalled for, and Henry needs to be called out for it. There's no way he didn't know that shit wasn't going down.

Cole storms into the warehouse first, it's quiet which is weird. Freddy isn't in his normal spot.

"Where the fuck is everyone?"

I look around when I notice a light coming from the office down the hallway. "Down there, in the furthest office."

The closer we get we can hear muffled voices coming from behind the closed door. Dorian doesn't bother knocking, his patience is wearing thin. Pushing it open he stalls. Blocking Cole and I from entering.

"What the fuck is going on?" he raises his voice in a thunderous tone. Coles had enough of waiting and pushes past him.

"Who the fuck is this?" he spat out.

I take notice of Henry sitting at his desk, while someone else is sitting across from him. His hair is black, and his moss like eyes never leave mine. Then he smiles.

"So, these must be the enforcers." He rises sticking out his hand. "I don't mean to be rude. I'm Conrad."

I step forward shaking his hand, squeezing a little harder than usual. I hate meeting people crouching in my territory and this guy is screaming hardcore.

"I'm Nyx, this is Dorian and Cole."

"What the hell is going on Henry?" Cole narrowed his eyes at Conrad.

"Calm down, boys. I heard about what happened at James' congratulations by the way. I'm impressed things could've gone way different; I knew you three could handle it."

"Handle that? It was a fuckin' mess and you know it. You knew all along that James was skimming didn't you, you just didn't care. Any other jobs you care to tell us about before we go." Dorian places a hand on Cole to keep him from doing anything he'll regret later.

Henry waves us off, then he simply stands. "Remember when I said I would only introduce you to the person once they caught the person responsible for digging up the graves?"

I try to keep my expression blank. The taste of bile slowly rises in my throat, if this is true Catalina is caught.

"I did the job that you three couldn't I caught the digger last night. It was rather easy; they didn't even hear me sneak up on them."

Them? "What do you mean them? There were two?"

"Oh yes, and they are in the torture room right now." Conrad sounds too excited; his entire face is glowing.

I send a side eye to Cole, where I see him dig his phone out of his pocket. We follow Henry and Conrad into the hallway.

"Anything?" Dorian asked.

"It goes straight to voicemail, we'll if they haven't caught her, then who the fuck did they catch?" I mummer.

"To be honest, I don't care as long as it isn't her," Cole grunted out.

"I still like to know who this Conrad guy is, I've never seen nor heard of him before. He weirds me out," Dorian states. I would have to agree. Where did Henry find this guy?

The door to the torture room is open, when I see who's inside, I freeze. They are both tied to a chair bloodied and the 'them' they are referring to is Professor Adams, and Professor Davis. Two people associated with Catalina. Tortured enough and Professor Davis will squeal like a pig.

"How do you know it's them?" Cole asked.

"I found them in the cemetery, poking around a grave. It was dug up." Conrad kicks Professor Davis.

He jolts awake, looking around with wide eyes shaking his head. Conrad kicks Professor Adams awake next. He moans coming too slowly. When he spots us three he panics. Pulling against his restraints, yelling into his covered mouth.

Recognition plays in Professor Adams' eyes when he calms down, he stares at me then moves his eyes to the corner of the room, he does this a few times before I catch on. I casually scratch my head turning.

My eyes land on something, something very familiar.

A tan satchel with pins all over it. I only know one person with that bag. I turn back to the professor; he nods slightly letting me know she's gone. Now I understand why they were caught.

The question is where the fuck is she, and who the fuck has her?

TO BE CONTINUED...

ABOUT THE AUTHOR

C L Easton lives in Alberta, Canada with her husband and two children. She loves all things horror, whiskey, true crime and things that don't involve people. Her dark sense of humour shines in her books, and is the least bit of a romantic. Funny isn't it. She loves to procrastinate, so it's amazing she finished this book. Kidding. She works great under pressure.

Find her on.
instagram.com/authorcleaston
www.authorcleaston.com
or her reading group on Facebook.com CL Reading Group

ALSO BY

A HITMANS SERIES
MYLES

CARTER

RUSSO MAFIA
UNBROKEN

STRANGERS OF EASTWOOD
STRANGERS OF THE NIGHT

Printed in Great Britain
by Amazon